EXECUTOR

EXECUTOR

LOUISE CARSON

Doug Whiteway, Editor

© 2015, Louise Carson

Cover design by Doowah Design.

Acknowledgements
The poems "The Key" and "Strange" were published online in *The Puritan* in 2013. "Small poems to the Chinese government" was recorded for a CD produced by Broken Rules Press, Sainte-Anne-de-Bellevue, Quebec, in 2014.

This book was printed on Ancient Forest Friendly paper.
Printed and bound in Canada by Hignell Book Printing Inc.

We acknowledge the support of the Canada Council for the Arts and the Manitoba Arts Council for our publishing program.

Library and Archives Canada Cataloguing in Publication

Carson, Louise, 1957-, author
        Executor / Louise Carson.

Issued in print and electronic formats.
ISBN 978-1-927426-67-8 (pbk.).--ISBN 978-1-927426-68-5 (html)

        I. Title.

PS8605.A7775E94 2015   C813'.6   C2015-901502-2
                                               C2015-901503-0

Signature Editions
P.O. Box 206, RPO Corydon, Winnipeg, Manitoba, R3M 3S7
www.signature-editions.com

To Mum,
who loved a good mystery

PROLOGUE

The old woman threw the scissors out the window, then shuffled from one area to another in her modest apartment, the plastic bag in one hand, the tape in the other. The bag bore the name of a national supermarket chain and its slogan: You Want It — We Have It! It was a soothing pale blue colour and dragged softly against her leg as she paced. The tape was that wide super-sticky stuff — great for securing packages.

The phone rang. Finally. She put the tape down on the desk and answered. As she spoke, the fingers of her left hand kneaded the bag's thin plastic where it lay on her knee. She hung up.

She didn't want to die — not like this, not in spring, her favourite season, summer's potential ahead. But the other, more known horror of that particular disease — that was no way either. She replayed the scene at the hospital: the exact moment when she'd known. She sighed and put the bag down next to the tape. She would make some tea.

As she waited for the kettle to boil she stood at the kitchen window and looked out at the afternoon. Green everywhere. Even the neighbour's high privacy fence, so typical in Toronto, separating their narrow backyards, was covered in ivy or creeper up and over the top. She looked more closely. Five leaves, palmate, so, creeper.

Her thoughts turned to the poems lying quietly in their files. Poems like fingers, she thought, grouped to form hands, the hands joined to the main body of work by her brain, her sensitivities and experiences. It was a good manuscript and would make a good book. After her death, she supposed. One way or another.

She made tea and set the stove timer for four minutes as she usually did. She liked her tea strong. She got out the milk and sugar.

—

For at least the tenth time the young man reread what he had typed into the computer. He was sure of his facts but still only half-believed them. A year ago he would have scoffed at some of the things he'd since discovered or guessed at. But even if they were only partly true, people had a right to know. His people. He didn't care about the others, was only using them as the best way to bring the information out. It would rebound from their countries back into his. Yet he hesitated to send. Probably, for him, it meant the end of everything.

He got up and went from the small grey room into the adjacent bathroom, checked his supplies. Shaver, soap, hair dye, makeup. The clothes, all new, were already packed. He decided to alter his appearance first and then send the document.

He removed all his clothing and began. First he shaved his body, all of it, from his eyebrows to his toes. He dyed his crewcut blond and made up his face, pencilling in a thin gold line above each eye. He checked the new face in the mirror. Now he looked like one of the moneyboys he'd observed in the sleazier of the Shanghai bars he'd visited last night. He shuddered fastidiously as he remembered the activities seen and offered in one bar's toilet. A far cry from his idea of love. He remembered his last lover and the face in the mirror softened. He decided to leave the building in the clothes he had been wearing the previous night, the scoop-necked white T-shirt and tight jeans further blurring his identity. Neither the clothes nor the previous night's venues were what was expected of him. He'd change into his jogging outfit at the run.

He carefully tidied up everything that related to him, packing the garbage from the two hotel wastebaskets in a plastic bag. He'd gradually get rid of it here and there.

He stood over the computer for the last time and pressed send, deleted, then overwrote the file. That should slow down any file restoration expert the authorities might employ. The computer was new and had been purchased for this purpose only. He didn't care if they retrieved the file anyway; he wanted people to know. It was just in case the email had been blocked from leaving the country that he'd bothered to delete the document at all. He needed time to effect his backup plan.

It was early evening as he slipped from the hotel into the street.

PART ONE

1

It had been a literary funeral, not unexpected, considering the fame of the dead woman. Poet, writer, activist, they had called her in their various eulogies. Peter himself had risen to recall his times with Eleanor; she the professor, he the student who became one of her teaching assistants before moving on and away to a career elsewhere. He'd spoken with respect of an exacting mentor, with affection of a kind friend.

He'd left out the semester when they'd been more than friends and colleagues to each other. That relationship had been short-lived, and, he believed, private. They'd found the thirty-year age difference at first exhilarating and then limiting.

Those guests who hadn't left directly after the service were standing or sitting in the spacious living room of Eleanor's daughter's house. The daughter, Dorothy Brandon-Hyde, known as Dot, after clutching one tissue after another at the funeral home, had composed herself and was offering plates of sandwiches and cups of coffee. She was still wearing the black dress she'd chosen for the funeral but, once home, had added an incongruous bright blue sweater.

Small and blonde, a little younger than Peter, she was a scholar herself — something in the humanities, he believed — and married to a banker. Her husband and children were circulating and didn't seem too affected by Eleanor's death, not if their smiling and even laughing with one guest or another was anything to judge them by. Some people, he knew, grieved in private. He was still waiting for his own reaction.

"Oh, Peter, thank you for coming," Dot breathed. Her hand in his was small and cold. "Would you care for a slice of cake?"

"Did you bake it, Dot?" he asked, taking a chunk. It looked good: pound cake with chocolate chips. It was good.

"No," said Dot. "One of the neighbours, I think. People have been so kind and I've been too busy with…" She trailed off, gulping. "Oh, Peter, what was she thinking? To do that."

He considered. "She always said she would, you know, if she got a terrible diagnosis."

"Yes, but there's a big difference between saying it and doing it. My grandmother, not Mum's mother but Dad's, used to say, 'Just take me out and shoot me if I start to get gaga,' but she didn't mean it."

"And did she? Get gaga?"

"Lived to ninety-one, then just turned her face to the wall, refused food, you know? Dead in a couple of weeks."

"Well, good for her. A determined lady. Like Eleanor." He changed the subject. "How are the kids taking it? And Bill?"

Dot shrugged. "Oh, Bill. He's philosophical." They looked across the room where Bill Hyde, tall and elegant in his black suit, was having an earnest discussion with an older gentleman. Peter wondered if his own choice of the salt-and-pepper jacket with black shirt, tie and pants had been appropriate. Dot continued, "He reminds me she was seventy-five, had had a great life, was loved. The kids, I don't know. Teenagers. They appear unconcerned and then…"

"I wouldn't know. My two are still small."

"Yes, I was forgetting. You got off to a late start, didn't you?"

Peter winced. "If you mean a failed first marriage followed by an infertile second, then yes, late." He paused. "Actually, I'm leaving for China shortly — adopting a third."

"Really? How interesting. Most people nowadays seem to feel two sufficient. Excuse me, I see I'm being signalled to by Bill. Don't leave, okay? There's something we have to discuss."

"I won't," he replied to her back. Now what could this be about, he thought? Choosing a memento from among Eleanor's books?

The crowd was thinning. Peter sat down on the sofa and watched people saying their goodbyes.

He didn't mind being alone at social functions. He'd had enough practice during the fifteen years between the end of one marriage and the beginning of the other. Eleanor and he had gotten together shortly after his divorce from Rachel. He realized he hadn't thought about Rachel in years. How different his life would have been if they'd stayed together. He tried to imagine it. She was a nurse, had supported him through his postgraduate degrees, and wanted children as soon as they'd married. But he kept delaying and when, by their late twenties, he'd finished his studies, she'd found someone else to be with.

And, to be honest, he'd already been attracted to Eleanor while still married. After her, except for brief relationships, he'd been one of the "solitaries" people invited to parties, the occasional dinner. Fifteen years of wondering if he'd done with real intimacy, fifteen years of depression, of wondering if what he needed was a therapist. And then his marriage to Jan and her revelation that she was infertile but wanted children.

He smiled as he thought of the girls: Jenny and Liza. They were so full of life and so strong-willed. Even at four and three years old they were a team — Jenny showing Liza how to eat, how to speak English. And Jan had expanded her already warm personality to include them along with Peter. About adopting a third, she said, "There's enough love to go around." And Peter could only agree.

He realized just Eleanor's family was left: Dot, of course, and a few older people, contemporaries of Eleanor. Her two children had gone elsewhere in the house. Bill Hyde was now offering drinks to the remaining guests. Peter stood up as the tall old man

Bill had been speaking with approached and shook his hand. Peter felt and then saw the slight tremor that pervaded the man's body.

"I'm James Cooper, Eleanor's cousin and her lawyer. I know you're Peter Forrest. It's good you're here. I have something to tell you, if now is a good time."

"Yes, of course. Here?"

"Yes. Dot and Bill will join us in a minute." The two men sat down. "Firstly, just to let you know, we've read the will and everything goes to Dot. Secondly, you are named as Eleanor's literary executor. Do you know what that means?"

Peter sat back. "I suppose it means I read any material she left, sort it, decide if it's publishable and archive the rest."

"You've got it, at least the obvious stuff."

"What else is there?"

"Well, you'd be managing the literary estate for the heir, Dot, and, as such, would be in a position of trust. There may be income from anything that is published. It was Eleanor's, and is Dot's wish, that you be reimbursed for your time and expenses."

"I see. I think I would have to know what amount of material is involved before I make a commitment. And I'd have to discuss it with my wife."

"Of course, of course. Do you live near Toronto?"

"I'm in Dunbarton, a couple of hours away by car, but work at York University a few days a week so I'm used to commuting and bringing work back to my house."

"What I meant was, can you stay in town now so I can show you Eleanor's papers and so on?"

"Oh." Peter spoke slowly. "Well, I suppose I could stay one night and go home tomorrow. It is a holiday weekend."

"So it is. The Queen's birthday. Time was, that would have been an excuse for a champagne toast while we watched the fireworks. I'd forgotten." The lawyer smiled ruefully. "I'm semi-retired and a bit out of the mainstream of activity. Would tomorrow morning work for you? I could leave you at the apartment for a few hours and then maybe you'd know if it was something you could take on."

"Tomorrow morning, then. I'll meet you there."

"Oh, you know where it is." Something shifted in Cooper's face.

"Well, yes, she'd been there for years, hadn't she?" For some reason, Peter felt defensive.

As the lawyer stood up, Peter could see Dot and Bill edging over.

James turned to them. "Peter's coming over to Eleanor's apartment tomorrow, Dot, and he'll let us know if he thinks he's the one for the job."

Dot appeared flustered. She pulled the blue sweater closed in front, folded her arms and hunched. "Shouldn't I be there?" Bill put an arm around her but she shrugged it off.

Oh, oh, thought Peter. He tried to sound reassuring. "Dot, I won't be looking at anything in depth, just trying to get an idea of the quantity, not the quality or content. Is Eleanor's computer there? If so, I'll need the password."

"Oh, I don't know the password. Does that mean we can't get into the files?"

"Don't worry. She may have written it down somewhere. And I won't remove any paperwork, or if I do, I'll clear it with James first."

Dot nodded, her face sagging with exhaustion. He took his leave, refusing offers of supper or a bed, made his way to a mid-range hotel and booked in. He went out again, got some Greek take-out and ate it in his room. Then he called Jan.

During the drive to Eleanor's apartment the next morning, Peter mulled over the conversation he had had with Jan the previous night. He'd first looked up what was involved in becoming a literary executor and realized that what he had imagined were the duties were just the beginning.

Besides physically sorting the material, he would be expected to balance Eleanor's wishes with Dot's — wishes that might be incompatible. As the gatekeeper to access, he would also have to deal with any would-be biographers, unless he were to attempt a biography of Eleanor himself. And he would handle requests from editors seeking to publish her work posthumously.

He'd relayed this information to Jan, who'd said that he should consider carefully before accepting such a trust. "Very time-consuming," had been her cogent remark. "And on top of your other work," she'd added, "and a new daughter." Promising to delay any decision, he'd thoughtfully hung up.

Yes, his other work. That was the problem: his other work wasn't really happening. Oh sure, he was teaching. But the poems had dried up. After twenty or more years of a small but steady output, they'd just stopped. And he didn't even know if anyone but he realized. He still had unpublished old poems to offer anthologies or magazines. But his last book had been seven or eight years ago and he knew one needed a lot of poems before a coherent manuscript could emerge.

Why not devote some time to Eleanor's literary legacy? It could be a good thing, give him a break from his anxiety about creating. He remembered one of Eleanor's sayings about writer's block. "When you can't write, write." He'd tried following it but had given up when he'd reread the mundane, even fatuous things he found his poetry saying.

He'd kept his eyes on the street signs for the last few minutes. Here it was, a side street south of Bloor, a little past Bathurst, on the left: an attractive building in which Eleanor had had an apartment on the second floor. There was no sign of James Cooper so he let himself in the unlocked outer door and walked upstairs. The door of the apartment before Eleanor's was open and in the doorway an elderly woman struggled with a lamp and a chair. Her hair was thin and straggly but she looked strong. Peter couldn't tell if she was coming or going but asked if she needed help.

She put down the chair and the lamp and gave him her attention.

"Who are you?" she asked. When he said he was a friend of Eleanor's, she commented, "Terrible, just terrible. We've been neighbours for the last ten years. A lovely woman. Private, but you could tell she was kind. Are you her son?"

Peter smiled and shook his head.

"Oh, yes, you said. A friend. My memory." She shook her head ruefully. "Her other friend has been here for a while." She paused. "Was it you called the day she killed herself?"

"Someone called? You mean telephoned?"

"Yes. Just before she killed herself, judging by how soon after that the ambulance people arrived. I wonder who called them."

"How did you know it was her telephone and not one in one of the other apartments?"

"I've been listening to that ring for ten years. We share a wall." She pointed to the interior of her apartment, the mirror image of Eleanor's.

Peter looked in politely and saw boxes and wrapping paper. "Are you moving?"

The woman made a face. "Yup. The big move. From an apartment to a retirement home. You never think it'll happen to you and then it does."

"Well, I should be going. Good luck with your move." Peter continued down the hall to Eleanor's door. It too was open and he saw James Cooper seated in a comfortable chair reading a book. The lawyer was again wearing a suit but it was blue today.

"One of yours, I believe," he said with a smile.

Peter took the book and read the inscription. "To dear Eleanor, who always has time for me. Love, Peter." He swallowed. The lawyer was looking at him with interested eyes.

"It's difficult, I know," Cooper said. "One feels one's own mortality as well as her loss." He gestured at the space. "Does it seem the same to you?"

Peter looked around the combination sitting, dining, office and kitchen area and nodded. "More or less. I haven't been here in more than fifteen years. When I was young."

The lawyer smiled grimly. "Those are frightening words the first time one hears them coming out of one's own mouth." He rose. "Well, I'll leave you to it. I have this for you." He reached into an inner pocket and produced a small envelope. "It was in with the will. I have a duplicate but this copy is for you. To keep." He offered it to Peter. As it shook in the air between them, Cooper looked at his own hand with what seemed like distaste. "Three hours enough? And then maybe lunch? Good."

Peter listened as Cooper closed the door and went down the stairs. He moved to the street side window and watched the lawyer drive away. Then, feeling a bit like someone who's just moved into a furnished apartment, he fumbled in the kitchen looking for what he needed to make a mug of something. He couldn't drink coffee without cream or at least milk and there was nothing in the fridge. He found a carton of preserved milk up in a cupboard but the scissors weren't in any of the drawers. Odd. He went over to Eleanor's desk. A slender Chinese vase held a small blunt-tipped pair buried among pens and pencils. Finally he carried coffee and letter to the table and sat.

The letter was typed and Peter smiled as he looked over at Eleanor's desk where the typewriter sat. Not that it was an old one: manufacturers still made typewriters for some reason. Maybe for countries where the Internet hadn't yet penetrated or where it was too expensive for most. And Eleanor had obviously still found hers useful for some tasks.

It was a beautiful letter. In it Eleanor had tried to set out her beliefs and goals and her thankfulness for having lived in a time and place that had allowed her to achieve so much of what she'd wanted. She pointed out to Peter that he was similarly blessed. And then she admonished him, ever so gently, not to forget the others, who she called "the unidentified." And she ended by hoping that he would be guided to use her writings in an appropriate fashion.

It was all a bit vague for Peter. He wondered who "the unidentified" were. A specific group or just in general? Yet he was moved. She'd tried to be a force for good. He took his coffee and walked into the bedroom.

It had been repainted since his time. He remembered blues and greens, had once remarked that he felt underwater there when a certain light filtered through the gauzy curtains. The walls now were painted a warm cream; the bedclothes were gold, the curtains brown. He remembered the room as a glorious mess with clothes strewn and books stacked on every surface, a place where he could be a lover, no more, no less; where they could drink wine in bed and argue about their favourite poets. This present room looked calm and organized and, he thought, a little sad. He finished his coffee and moved back into the main area of the apartment, and to the desk, which held her typewriter, laptop and some odds and ends: little trays and boxes for the tools of the writer's trade — stamps, paper clips — and the yellow vase with its contents. He slid open a drawer. Receipts for books and paper, more stamps, a list of monies received for lectures, a few small notebooks with rough notes for poems, sometimes merely a single line, underlined.

Nothing unexpected here. He slid open the desk's deep file drawer and took out the first three files.

File one contained a list of publishers of magazines and books, with notes on who to approach and what they were like. He grinned as he read some of the candid assessments. "Fancies himself" was next to one name while "Bully" appeared next to another. That would be fun to read. He returned it to the drawer.

File two seemed to contain the text of a lecture she'd prepared: "Chinese poetry and censorship in the twentieth century." He put that aside to take home to read.

File three was thicker than the others and contained the notes from which file two's essay had been prepared, as well as dossiers on specific Chinese poets and some of their translated work. Into the read-at-home pile it went.

He turned his attention to the computer. Password, password. He looked around the room, then typed in two names: those of the two grandchildren he'd met at the funeral. He reversed the names, put in a hyphen, then an oblique between them. Nothing.

No pets in Eleanor's life, so that was out. He tried Dot's name, Dot and Bill's together, even, sheepishly, his own. No. He left it for now and investigated the filing cabinet next to the desk. Two drawers, both full. This time he pulled out the three last files in the bottom drawer.

Ah. Poems. Each one was a slender column, a few words on the page. Each file held about twenty-five, neatly typed out. Sections for a book, he thought, and became engrossed reading. He was startled by Cooper appearing at the door.

"Well?"

"Well," said Peter, replacing the poems he'd read and adding one more unread file to the small pile on the desk. "I'll take these, if I may."

"Certainly, certainly. Are you any closer to a decision?"

"I'd like a few days," answered Peter. "You said something about lunch, Mr. Cooper?"

"My treat, and do call me James. Do you like Greek food?"

"Love it," smiled Peter. "Love it."

Back in the chaos of a home life with two toddlers but in the relative peacefulness of the small town where the family lived,

Peter spent a few days reading the files he'd brought home and thought about what it might mean if he took on this task. He could see several streams of endeavour.

Eleanor the poet was going to be a dream to administer. She had at least one book prepared and other poems from which to possibly make another. Peter would edit, write an introduction, and then the poems would make their own way in the world as poems did.

Eleanor the activist was more complicated. She seemed to hold a watching brief for many dissident poets, mostly from China. Notes were appended and dated to individuals' files, many of which contained disturbing entries. "Last seen at University of — ." "Last published in — Magazine." Peter wasn't sure he had the desire or the methodology to update the activities of poets on the other side of the world.

"Daddy!" screamed Jenny, rushing into his study and throwing herself at him. Behind and a little lower down he heard "Da-dee!" as Liza copied her sister and clasped his leg on his other side.

"Daddy, we bought groceries."

"Zozeries," echoed Liza.

Jenny corrected her. "Grrrroceries, Liza, like a growling bear. Grrrr!" She chased the pleasantly terrified Liza from the room as Jan entered it. She was of average height and build, her hair was wavy and medium brown, her face unremarkable, yet he looked at her with pleasure, as he usually did. Her unfailing good nature made their lives work.

She leaned over him, giving him a kiss. "How's it going, hon? Help me with lunch?"

As they made grilled cheese sandwiches and heated up soup, Peter described what the job of being Eleanor's literary executor would involve. And then he talked about what it could involve: the activism.

As they ate, he said, "It's not me, you know, not really. I love language and logic and connection. I've never been an altruist. Should I do it if my heart's not in it?"

Jan replied, handing Liza her sandwich cut into thin strips. "To me it doesn't seem as though the activism is necessarily a part of the literary executorship. Am I right?"

"Ye-es. But according to Eleanor's letter, it's her wish for that work to continue."

The sound of a flush and then a wail came from the bathroom next to the kitchen, where Jenny was relieving herself. "I dropped the toilet paper!" was her shrill cry. Peter rescued her and jiggled the handle till the toilet calmed.

"When is that guy supposed to come and fix this bathroom?" he asked Jan irritably.

"In July. He didn't say exactly when. Peter, why not contact someone who is an activist? Or an organization? Maybe they'd know someone else who could take on that political stuff?"

Peter smiled at his wife. "Great idea. And you, are you fine with me doing the literary part?"

"Of course, sweetie. You'll be good at it. Now, who wants ice cream?"

With cries of "Me, me" reverberating in his ears, Peter went to telephone his acceptance to James Cooper.

2

Peter half rose from his window seat and the nervous couple next to him slid sideways, stood and let him out. They were both stocky, like him, more challenged by the width of the airplane seats than the lack of legroom. He made it to the aisle and stretched. He'd be glad to be free of them for a few minutes, tired of their constant mutual reassuring. "Do you think she'll cry? They say they usually cry. If she cries, I'll cry." "You're allowed to cry. I just hope she's not afraid of me, you know, men. I'll give her a toy right away, don't you think?" "We have to bond, we just have to. What if we never bond?"

Peter had feigned interest in the plane's music and movie, had slept and meditated, but when the husband of the couple had turned and asked directly if he, Peter, was going to China on business, Peter hadn't had the heart to say yes, had admitted that he was returning for his third child. And had been flooded by a cascade of questions about procedure and paperwork, who to tip and not to tip, as well as the inevitable "and how are the children you already have?" to which he was able to respond with certainty and a smile that "they're great, really great." He'd described vivacious Jenny and loving little Liza.

Later, during one of those lulls between the various services the cabin crew provided during long flights, he walked slowly around the cabin. He found a space between one of the bathrooms and the last row of seats in the plane's mid-section and did some slow stretches and leg and arm lifts. Then he went to the bathroom. Then he walked around a bit more.

Third time lucky, he thought idly, then self-corrected; third time still lucky. Jenny and Liza had helped him choose and pack gifts for the new sister, though he doubted Liza had a clear idea of what was happening. Jenny, on the other hand, had been through this before and had her own thoughts on what were appropriate gifts and equipment. Jammed into Peter's bag were a blanket, a stuffed toy cat and several packs of her favourite candy — hard, fruit-flavoured and shaped like a pacifier. When the kids watched a movie at home, they each had one, loudly straining melting sugar through their milk teeth in a way that would have made the family dentist shudder if she could have seen and heard it. Peter and Jan brushed the kids' teeth carefully those nights.

He thought about Jan. She'd been his "date" at one of those dinner parties married couples often invited him to. He'd been attracted to her obvious warmth and cheerful laugh. She was thirty-seven to his forty, from eastern Ontario originally — a country girl. It hadn't been long before they both realized the other was easy to be with and they fell in love.

Back at his seat, the anxious couple, the Stedmans, were conferring. The wife, Amanda, attractive with her medium-length dark hair, careful makeup, jewellery and colourful clothes, spoke. "Peter." She cleared her throat. "Peter, we wondered what district your baby is coming from." He mentioned Fujian province, southwest of Shanghai, and the city of Fuzhou, its capital, and knew by their looks of relief that it was the same place to which they were headed. "Oh good," she said, "someone to be with." He didn't point out that they, in fact, didn't know him, that they were from a different city and province back in Canada than his, and that after they got their child they'd probably neither want nor need his assistance. They'd have, as he would have, a guide provided by the adoption agency who would translate, ensure they made all their appointments and even take them around to tourist sights.

Peter thought back to their first trip to China: he and Jan going for Jenny. They'd been pretty quiet, each lost, he supposed, in contemplating the seriousness of the step — Jan in her late thirties and Peter in his early forties, and Jenny, their soon-to-be daughter, just a little more than two years old, existing to them, so far, as a photograph in a file.

For Liza, Jan had felt confident enough to go by herself while Peter stayed home with Jenny. And now it was his turn to "fly" solo. He grinned, hearing Jan's parting words. "Make sure you get the right baby, Peter. And no twofers." They'd agreed this would be their last adoption.

During the fourteen-hour flight from Toronto to Shanghai he'd had ample opportunity to review the status of his work on Eleanor Brandon's literary estate.

Her apartment had been cleared out and a new tenant found. Her files and books, the ones he thought pertinent, were at Peter's home or his office at the university. He'd looked through everything once quickly while it was still in Toronto and had begun the laborious process of itemizing and classifying poems, notes and correspondences once the files had been removed. He never did figure out Eleanor's password but it turned out Dot had simply forgotten that, along with the spare keys to the apartment her mother had left with her while still alive, she'd included a USB key. Peter had downloaded what was on the key into his own computer and discovered not only Eleanor's password but all the same files her laptop contained. She had been a careful woman. And the password — compassion — was so Eleanor.

He'd also taken charge of, but been reluctant to read, the part of Eleanor's work that he classified as "activist." Neither had he passed it on to anyone else who might know better how to handle the material. In the excitement of planning for the China trip and adoption, he just hadn't had the time. Anyway, he figured Eleanor's literary output was more his field and that poems mattered too, not as much as people's lives, but they mattered. And he would honour Eleanor by taking meticulous care of them.

They touched down in Shanghai only to encounter a delay with their connecting flight south. Patiently, Peter settled himself at the flight gate with a coffee and watched the crowds of people. The Stedmans were dozing, worn out by anticipation and the long flight.

He felt fortunate to be going to Shanghai this time. The first trip, they had been based in Beijing and Jan had returned there when she had picked up Liza. Beijing was wonderful. The Summer Palace appealed: set amidst ponds and greenery, it was a good place to go with a young child. Visiting the different bits of the Great Wall near Beijing had been great too, if sweaty and crowded. He'd felt a qualm of negative emotion crossing Tiananmen Square but had enjoyed the subsequent tour of the Forbidden City. Those sites as well as visiting the *hutongs*, the traditional neighbourhoods, had easily used up the week it took to get Jenny's final exit papers sorted out. And now he looked forward to exploring Shanghai after the week in Fuzhou.

It wouldn't take long to get there. Fuzhou was about as far from Shanghai as Toronto was from Montreal, so an hour in the air should do it. He'd rather have taken the high-speed train but the adoption agency said the plane was more efficient, as he would already be at the airport.

He knew that Fuzhou was on a river, that it would be hot and humid, that his baby came from an orphanage up the river and that there was a strong Buddhist presence throughout Fujian province.

He woke with a start to find Josh Stedman shaking him gently by the shoulder. "Time to go, Peter. Peter, let's go." It had been almost twenty hours since they'd left home and they were, all three of them, starting to show it. Amanda had freshened her makeup and Josh had shaved around his beard and moustache. Peter felt a bit soiled by comparison but knew he'd be able to spruce up in the hotel room after what he hoped would be a long sleep. Once on the second airplane he resumed his doze. The warm wet towel the flight attendant distributed near the end of the flight felt terrific and he held it on his face as long as it retained its heat.

It turned out that the Stedmans and he were at the same hotel and would be sharing the same guide. Lin Huiyin was a serious-looking woman of about forty, dressed in navy slacks and blazer and a white shirt. Her shoes were sensible and her English was good. Just what we need, thought Peter. He didn't take in much during the taxi ride to the hotel, where he took a cursory shower before collapsing into a ten-hour sleep.

The next morning the four of them met in the glass-and-gold-metal-decorated hotel lobby and moved to a buffet breakfast in the adjacent dining room. The Stedmans were too excited to eat but Lin Huiyin enjoyed her rice and tea while Peter ate his way through a large plate of bacon, eggs and toast. On the way to the civil affairs office everyone was quiet, looking out the taxi windows at busy Fuzhou. It seemed a long ride to the jet-lagged, would-be parents, but in less than half an hour they'd reached their destination.

When they sat down in the waiting area in an airless hallway, Peter noticed that there was one other couple already there, softly speaking to each other in Spanish. In a few minutes they went in and Lin Huiyin told the Stedmans they were next and then Peter.

He pulled a notepad and pen out of his backpack and jotted down a few ideas he'd had for a poem. He was feeling just a hint of inspiration when the Spanish couple emerged with a crying girl who looked about one year old but was probably closer to two. The father was waving a toy while the mother clasped the child, herself in tears.

The Stedmans looked at Peter tentatively. He spoke in a low voice. "The kids go into shock when they have to say goodbye to their nanny from the orphanage. You just have to wait it out. Sometimes it takes a few hours before they realize they're not going back and then they have to let their feelings out. After that, it gets better. Really."

Lin Huiyin nodded her agreement, then went into the office with the Stedmans' papers.

"Do you have any candy?" Peter asked Josh. "Candy is good." Josh shook his head. Peter rummaged in the backpack for a candy pacifier and handed them two. "I have several and we can probably buy more here," he said.

Their guide appeared at the office door, beckoning the Stedmans. They both looked pale as they passed through the door. Peter knew he now had about an hour or more and returned to his notebook.

When Amanda and Josh reappeared they were clutching papers and a little girl, who was contentedly sucking away at the pacifier. "Thank you so much," said Amanda. "We'll see you later." Lin Huiyin had taken some of Peter's documents into the office and in a few moments ushered him in.

It was as hot as the hallway had been and small. There were five people waiting for him. He slid his eyes over them all, then directed his attention to the stern-looking official behind the desk. The questioning began, Lin Huiyin translating.

"Will you ever abandon this child?" "No." "What is your job exactly?" "I am a university professor of English literature." "Where do you live?" "I live in Dunbarton, Ontario, a small town east of Toronto, the largest city in Canada." "How long have you been married?" "I have been married for five years." "How much salary do you earn?" "I earn one hundred and fifteen thousand dollars a year." "Does your wife work?" "No." "Why not?" "She likes to stay at home with the children."

The official's assistant stood at the ready, presented the right paper at the right time and, after Peter signed, left the room to make copies. The questions and signings alternated. Peter was aware of the director of the orphanage sitting to one side while the child's nanny held his new daughter on her lap. There seemed to be an unspoken tension between the two women. The nanny especially appeared nervous.

During a lull in the questions, as the two officials conferred over their papers, Peter took a good hard look at the little girl, then made his decision.

When the red wax appeared, he knew they were nearly done. He pressed his thumb firmly into the soft material and watched as his daughter Annie was gently assisted to press her palm onto a larger amount. He signed some more papers. And then it was time for the money, the donation to the orphanage. He laid the package on the desk and felt their combined attention shift from him to it. He opened the package and fanned the red one-hundred-yuan bills. Quietly he said, "Three thousand American dollars."

All that was left to do was to present the gifts. For the impeccably dressed orphanage director he had a bottle of Canadian whisky and for the official behind the desk Canadian cigarettes.

Everyone stood up and shook hands, then Peter sat back down as the nanny brought him the child. He opened his backpack, taking his time, and brought out the blanket. He looked at Annie, then shook his head, putting the blanket on his lap. He thought, as he shook his head, he heard a small sound from the nanny. He rummaged again, this time producing a small book. He held it up, then again shook his head, placing the book on the blanket. Now he knew he had the baby's attention, he brought out a stuffed toy — the cat Jenny had packed — and slowly extended it in the baby's direction, handing it to the child's nanny, who spoke encouragingly to her charge before passing on the toy. Finally Peter produced his secret weapon, the candy pacifier, and pretended to suck on it, saying "Yum, yum." At this point the nanny put the child on her feet and helped her wobble over to Peter. As the little hand closed on the candy, the nanny released a soft sigh. Peter swiftly rose and left the room with his daughter.

He waited in the hallway for Lin Huiyin and they took a taxi back to the hotel. "If we can just make it back to the room," Peter smiled to the guide. "Hopefully," she replied. Fortunately, Annie was interested in looking out the window and sucking her candy and it wasn't until she was alone in the hotel room with Peter that the crying began. He turned on the television with the volume set low and let her become distracted while he fiddled around with tidying his things and putting out clothes and diapers for her.

That first day they ate and napped in the room until evening when Peter phoned Jan. "It went well. She's sleeping, I don't know for how long. She doesn't look anything like her picture. She's much thinner than we thought she'd be and she doesn't walk much for her age. How are the girls? I miss you."

3

That night, as Peter tried to sleep, he kept imagining someone breaking into his house and harming Jan and the kids. And all for some information about dissidents. It seemed impossible that he and his family were now involved. He replayed that evening's phone call in his mind and tried to make sense of it.

"We miss you too, love. I can't wait to see Annie. Listen, someone from the university called to say your office has been broken into."

"What?"

"I know, weird, eh? Jenny, stop teasing Liza. Eat your breakfast. Anyway, Ted whatever-his-name is, the guy in the office next to yours, noticed the door was open and knew you were away so checked — and guess what?"

"What?"

"They took the office computer. That's it."

Peter was silent.

"Hon?"

"Yeah, what?"

"All you keep saying is 'what?' So, campus security called the police and the police were here and were asking whether you might have any sensitive material in there, anything they should know about. I told them to ask you. I think it's students or maybe just regular thieves looking for something to sell."

"Oh, God, this might be about Eleanor's activities. I knew I didn't want to get mixed up in this. Okay. I want you to give the police all Eleanor's stuff that's not related to her own poetry. I've kept it pretty separate. It's in the study. It shouldn't be too difficult to sort. And, Jan, do it soon. I'm worried about this."

"Oh, Peter, for heaven's sake, calm down. Nothing's going to happen in Dunbarton. Bye. Love you."

The next morning, when he awoke exhausted, Peter would have loved to have been able to turn over and go back to sleep but Annie was hungry. He gave her a cookie, showered himself and gently bathed her. He put on shorts and comfortable shoes and dressed Annie in a cute little matching top and pants his mother-in-law had bought for her on which giraffes cavorted, contorting their necks, then carefully carried her down to breakfast. The Stedmans were already there — all three of them. Josh was cutting up a banana while a beaming Amanda handed Julia the pieces.

"Rough night?" asked Josh.

"Yeah," grunted Peter, "but Annie was fine. I was worried about some stuff happening at work my wife just told me about. Now, what's for breakfast, young lady?" He pointed at the banana and Annie nodded. He carried her to the buffet and, while she watched, selected a few things he thought she might like, then solemnly fed her. When she was done, he went back and got himself a plate.

"We thought we might go up the river," said Josh. "It's hot but there might be a breeze on the water."

"Yeah, that sounds nice," said Peter absently.

Lin presented herself at their table shortly thereafter and they asked about the river. She thought that would be a good plan and easy to arrange after they visited the notary for more documentation. She explained that it would take the rest of the week for all the paperwork to be assembled.

By eleven that morning they found themselves on a medium-sized tour boat, motoring up the Min. Downtown Fuzhou was flat but once they were on the water they saw first a row of hills behind the city and then a row of mountains higher up. The slopes were tree covered with rocky patches showing here and there.

"Mount Fu," said Lin, pointing at one mountain. "It gives its name to Fuzhou, which means 'the blessed settlement.' There are many ancient temples here and in the whole province of Fujian."

So much for the preconception that religion is oppressed in China, thought Peter.

That Fuzhou was a busy and wealthy city was apparent from the number of luxury apartment buildings and shopping malls that lined the river and continued inland into the heart of the city. "Very expensive to live here," said Lin. "You should go shopping, take a walk along the river another day."

As they left behind the industrial outskirts of Fuzhou, the river narrowed and small towns replaced the big city's commercial skyline with their more natural-looking ones. The sky clouded over and a fine mist descended, first over the distant mountains, then covering the nearer hills, finally obscuring the nearby shores and creeping over the water. The temperature dropped slightly and Amanda shivered.

"I think we should go back. It's too damp."

Privately, Peter was enchanted. The boat's rocking motion had lulled Annie to sleep in the baby sling he was wearing and he was enjoying the stillness on the water. It was nice not to be in a city and the air felt cool and comfortable on his skin.

"We can land soon," said Lin. "Maybe get some lunch. It'll be warm in the restaurant. See? Over there."

They could just make out some low structures against the landscape and, as they grew nearer, a few small boats at anchor.

Lin spoke. "Either that or we stay on the boat and return to Fuzhou."

"I'm hungry," said Josh, "and we do want to sightsee." He looked at Amanda.

Peter agreed. "I could eat. Authentic Fujian food, I hope." He smiled at Amanda.

"Very authentic," Lin replied. "Very fresh."

Both babies were awake now and Amanda nodded her agreement. "I need to change her diaper and I can't see doing that on the boat. When is the next boat back to Fuzhou?"

"In about two hours. We'll have lunch and maybe walk a little." Lin looked pleased and, now that they'd left the city, more relaxed. Peter imagined that she must enjoy her job; there was lots of freedom, even pleasure, in taking tourists around.

As the boat approached the steps that descended the jetty, they could see the ten or so people waiting for the return trip to Fuzhou approach the tip of the pier. The boat pulled up alongside and, after it was tied up, the passengers aboard alighted carefully onto the nearest step and walked up to the pier.

Peter and the others passed the people waiting to take their places on the boat: the elderly, students, a couple of children — none of whom seemed interested in the Westerners. Lin led them down the main street of the village to a small restaurant. The smell of fish was strong and delicious. Lin ordered for them and soon the dishes appeared: dumplings first, then fish, shrimp and vegetables in broth. The food was neither bland nor spicy hot but light, fragrant. There was little speaking as everyone ate appreciatively.

They had time to wander the little town, which seemed a quiet backwater, and was made up of little more than a few houses, a grocery shop and the restaurant. Peter replenished his supply of cookies and candy in the store and then it was time to catch the boat for the return trip.

During the ride he handed out small pieces of the peanut candy Lin said Fujian province was famous for. The mist lessened and the sky brightened. They were quiet as the boat motored down the Min.

In the hotel lobby they discussed the next day's possibilities. Josh and Amanda were content to stay in Fuzhou, maybe shop for gifts to bring home. Peter asked Lin if he could go to the city of Annie's origin and photograph her orphanage, in order to create some kind of record for her to look at in the future. Lin said she would let him know the next morning and left for the day.

Just in case he went, Peter asked the Stedmans if they would like to have two babies for a day.

Amanda looked doubtful. "Aren't you worried that she'll miss you or that you'll disrupt any bonding that's going on?"

"I'm more worried about her seeing her home and friends and having to disconnect all over again if I bring her with me." Peter handed Annie to Josh. The baby immediately put her hands on Josh's moustache. "She's tickling me," he laughed.

"I'll go to the toilet for a few minutes and you can see if she notices I'm gone," said Peter, heading to the ones at the far end of the hotel lobby. After waiting a few extra minutes he washed his hands and splashed cold water on his face.

When he returned to the lobby he didn't immediately retrieve Annie, who was happily squeaking with Julia while Josh and Amanda jiggled and supported their respective babies.

"What do you think? Can you cope? I'll fly so it should be a brief trip. I only want to view the orphanage and a bit of the surrounding area. Take some pictures to make her a scrapbook when we get home."

The Stedmans looked at each other then burst out laughing — a little hysterically, Peter thought.

"I don't suppose I could be any more exhausted than I already am," said Josh.

"Nobody tells you how tired your arms will get," added Amanda. "It's like lifting weights, but the weights have a will of their own."

Peter retrieved Annie. "See you tomorrow at breakfast," he said. "And thanks."

Peter wasn't hungry, so he and Annie nibbled fruit and cookies instead of supper. While he waited to call Jan, he thought of various words or phrases he could use to let her know what he suspected, but decided she'd only worry. Better wait until they returned home. Meanwhile he would have to keep his cool. For Annie's sake, if not for his own.

So he told Jan about their newest daughter, the beautiful trip up the river, the great lunch, the Stedmans' and his plans for the next day.

He awoke at six, not to the sound of his alarm ringing but to the ringing of the hotel phone. It was Lin. He could go to Annie's orphanage but the flight left shortly. He would be met on his arrival by another guide who would drive him.

He hurriedly changed and dressed Annie, then went along to the Stedmans' room where he kissed her and handed her over to a sleepy Josh, muttering, "Thanks a million," and left.

He ate on the plane: tea and a bun. A thick cloud cover prevented him from seeing much landscape during the short flight but, as he knew Fujian province was mostly mountainous, he wasn't surprised that when the small airport appeared during the plane's descent, it seemed entirely surrounded by forested hills.

He went down the staircase next to the plane and crossed the tarmac. Inside the terminal Peter was met by a young man in grey dress pants and a long-sleeved white shirt buttoned up to the neck, holding a piece of paper on which Peter's name was written.

"I am Chen," he said.

"Just Chen?" Peter smiled, knowing the Chinese preference for using full names, at least during introductions.

"Just Chen. Driver. Translator. This way, please." He walked briskly to a waiting car.

Different, thought Peter, getting in beside the man. "Better view in front," he murmured. No reply. Right, he thought, and looked out the window.

The city was placed in an area where low hills were interrupted by the river basin, the same river that flowed past Fuzhou. But up here, in the mountains, it had many tributaries and so the city contained many bridges, and mingled with the sound of traffic was that of rushing water. Far in the distance and high up, a slender waterfall gushed down a rock face.

Chen drove silently. So, not a guide, thought Peter, but what he said, a driver. Suits me. I'm not asking any questions anyway. I'm here to take pictures.

They pulled up at a large, gated building and Chen parked outside on the street. Peter took a picture out the window at some buildings across the street from the orphanage.

"Your travelling papers, your passport?"

Peter handed them over to Chen. "Why?" he asked.

Chen replied, "Army likes to know when visitors on their street."

Peter's eyebrows lifted but Chen had already disappeared into the building just to the left of the orphanage gate.

Peter got out of the car and took a couple more pictures. The orphanage's walls were a pale creamy colour and its roofs were reddish-orange. There were balconies, open windows and rows of neatly tended plants in pots lined up either side of the entrance gate and dotted around the courtyard in front of the building. Peter thought it looked attractive and peaceful, an oasis away from the busier parts of the street. He could hear children. Part of the top storey seemed to open onto a gallery where laundry flapped. Behind the building a steep and green-covered hill rose.

Chen returned, gave back Peter's documents, and they walked through the gates. A woman in a white coat came to greet them and Chen performed introductions. Peter didn't recognize the woman as either the orphanage director or Annie's nanny. He offered an envelope with what Lin had suggested was the proper amount inside — a small donation to the orphanage, in thanks for the meeting. The woman's face was closed, empty as she bowed slightly, took the money and turned.

"No pictures inside the orphanage, please," said Chen. "And no pictures of children."

They walked up the three flights of stairs to the rooftop gallery. Peter took pictures of the landscape in the distance. Perhaps one day these scenes would resonate with Annie. He leaned over the railing and photographed some of the neighbouring properties, including the parking lot behind the military building next door. A large white van parked there seemed to be functioning as a portable office or something, as various tubes and wires connected it with the building. As they toured the facility, Peter tried to take mental pictures of the rooms and the furniture with their cheerful colours and the small low beds. It all seemed nice, very clean. Here children were playing, here having a snack. It was really—

An alarm bell began ringing and everyone moved — fast. "Fire," said Chen calmly. The children were guided into groups that waited their turn to exit the building. Chen and the woman went swiftly down a staircase, Peter following. The two Chinese had already pushed through the exit door to the outside when Peter heard a sound that caused him to look over his shoulder. Coming up the stairs from below were a half-dozen surgeons and nurses, gowned and masked, stripping off surgical gloves as they walked. Peter and they regarded each other with surprise, then all exited the building to the courtyard where the children were being assembled.

The next time Peter looked casually around, the surgical team had disappeared. "I guess the tour is over?" he asked Chen.

"Yes. We can't go back in. Kitchen fire." Chen seemed unfazed by the event as he ushered Peter back to the car. Nor did he comment on the soldiers from the building next door running with fire extinguishers through the door from which he and Peter had left the building.

Peter remarked blandly, "Oh, how kind, they're coming to help," and got into the car. He was sweating and trembling and muttered, "Must be shock," as Chen started the car and pulled away.

Back at the airport, Peter thanked Chen, then headed for the check-in counter. Once through security he bought a coffee and sat facing a window, watched the planes coming and going.

4

Over the next two days Peter tried not to think too much about what he had seen and what it might mean. Annie had seemed happy to see him when he returned and they had spent their remaining time in Fuzhou doing the tourist tours, sometimes with and sometimes without the Stedmans.

Peter especially enjoyed the ancient buildings in the district known as Three Lanes and Seven Alleys and ate some wonderful sweet and sour pork in a restaurant there. He took pictures of the Black Pagoda and of the White Pagoda and made a special trip to see the Jinshan Temple. Built on a slab out in the water, it made a striking sight with its red walls and pillars, white balcony railings and grey tile roof with protective horns. As always when around Eastern temples, he thought of Eleanor, how she would have loved to see such sights. As far as he knew she'd never been to Asia.

As Lin had suggested, he more than once strolled the riverside walkway of the upmarket Taijiang district where the wealthy of Fuzhou had their condominiums. Thinking of Jan and the girls at home, he bought lacquerware jewellery boxes and a medium-sized paper umbrella. Good thing he'd brought one suitcase half empty, he thought, as he packed the gifts the last night in Fuzhou.

The next morning he and the Stedmans said goodbye to Lin at the airport. She'd presented them with the final papers establishing adoption the previous day and, though he knew the adoption agency said tips to guides were included, Peter had given her an extra gift of money at that time. As they parted, he quipped, "halfway there" and waved Annie's little hand at her. Blank-faced, Lin held up her hand in a single gesture. Her attitude to Peter had changed since his day at the orphanage. No more smiling, and she'd kept her distance.

That evening he met Josh and Julia for supper in the Shanghai hotel where they were all staying.

"Where's Amanda?"

"She begged for a hot bath and an evening off," replied Josh. "I thought I'd go for a stroll after supper. Been sitting all day. Want to come?"

"I'd like that but just a quick one." Annie had just yawned. "I guess she can sleep in the sling."

The two men strolled a few blocks away from their hotel, looking at restaurants and nightclubs, seeing tourists going into some while the Chinese entered others.

"Kind of segregated," noted Josh.

"Just the language, I'd guess," said Peter, "and possibly different tastes in food or music."

"We'll never know," said Josh. "No nightlife for us."

"Not this trip anyway."

They passed a park where mostly men were hanging out.

"Do you think?" began Josh.

"I suppose. It's the same in Toronto. In the large parks or down by the water. Do you know Toronto?"

"Oh, yeah, been there to visit family." Josh paused. "Several of my cousins left Quebec when the P.Q. got in years ago. But Amanda's parents are still alive and property is so much cheaper in Montreal compared with Toronto. I have my own business. I doubt we'll move."

"We can't afford Toronto either. That's why we live in Dunbarton. It's a good thing I only have to be at work two or three times a week. The commute is a killer."

They were headed back to the hotel when they heard shouting. They turned to look and saw police running into the park while the other men tried to run out.

"Let's get going," said Peter.

"Is it illegal to be gay in China or are they soliciting in there?" asked Josh.

"I don't know. I think it's illegal. But that doesn't mean it isn't there."

"No, of course not."

They paused in the hotel lobby. By Josh's furrowed brow, Peter saw mirrored his own disquiet at what they had just witnessed. They said their goodnights.

The day they'd arrived in Shanghai, the new guide seemed pleasant: male, around thirty-five, small, round, and cheerful. He said his name was Wu Cheng but to call him Wu. And the next morning, when he'd knocked at Peter's door, he'd been all business, retrieving the necessary papers and specifying when Peter and Annie would be needed at the Canadian consulate later that day.

He suggested that as the day was hot and breezeless and the humidity high, the air pollution would be subsequently high and that Peter and Annie should stay indoors or only venture out briefly. He was gone before Peter thought to ask about air filtering masks. Anyway, he thought, they were only in Shanghai for six days. What kind of damage could be done in such a short time?

The Stedmans were spending a quiet day at the hotel: Julia had had a fussy night and they were exhausted. So after breakfast Peter and Annie walked out alone.

He quite liked his new daughter, found her calmness endearing as she rode around in the sling, taking in the sights and sounds of the world's largest city with him.

Wu had been right: the air was heavy. Many people wore masks and the sun was invisible above the fog of pollution, as was most of the river when they made their way to it.

"Not a good day for a river cruise," Peter said to Annie. They wandered along the walkway with other tourists. Peter felt comfortable hearing English and other European languages being spoken. Annie was squirming, so he let her walk a bit. She seemed healthy enough. When she tired, he scooped her up in his arms and held her there for the walk back to the hotel. Every few minutes he kissed the top of her head.

They ate their lunch in the restaurant at the front of the hotel, looking out at the street. As he ate his chicken and fat Shanghai noodles with pickled vegetables and fed Annie, he thought about what he had seen at the orphanage: the beautiful courtyard, the surgical team, the happy children, the soldiers next door. He knew he could do nothing while still in China. To raise questions here could delay Annie's and his exit from the country. And so far he had only vague suspicions. He wished he knew more about China.

Peter and Wu arrived at the Canadian consulate a little before three that afternoon. Annie had napped and, refreshed, was taking an interest in all that passed before her, though not that much was happening in the corridor where Peter and Wu were seated. Eventually Wu was called over by an official and they had a conversation while Peter watched and waited, trying to look unconcerned. After a few minutes Wu approached.

"They would like a meeting."

"Of course." Peter rose. "Is anything wrong?"

"I can't say," Wu replied.

I bet you can't, thought Peter, smiling amiably and following the official. This is your own government, he told himself. There's nothing to worry about. To his surprise, Wu sat back down in the corridor.

"Mr. Forrest? Would you come this way, please?"

He followed the official down several hallways until they paused outside a door. The young man knocked and entered. The older civil servant behind the desk rose and shook Peter's hand, gesturing for him to take a seat and brusquely waving the younger man away. Peter noticed the little Canadian flag pin in his left lapel.

The man spoke aggressively. "Mr. Forrest, my name is Macdonald and my job is to make sure Canadians in China have as little trouble with the authorities as possible."

"Am I in trouble?" Peter couldn't help it. His voice stuck and rasped in his throat. Annie looked up at his face.

"No, no. It's more a matter of confirming a report made by a third party about an incident at the orphanage you visited a few days ago in Fujian province. Could you tell us in your own words what happened there?"

So Peter spoke about Chen, the drive to the orphanage, the army-occupied building next door to the orphanage, how nice the orphanage looked, the fire there and their subsequent exit, how the soldiers had come to put out the fire and how he had then been driven back to the airport.

"And those things were all that you saw, all that struck you?" Macdonald looked sharply at Peter as he spoke.

Peter wished he knew whether the man wanted full disclosure for some reason of security or would just as rather he, Peter, kept quiet about seeing the surgeons come up from the orphanage basement. It was Annie who decided him. The most important thing now was to get her back to Canada.

"That's it. For an orphanage, I thought it was situated in a great spot, lots of plants and forest in the background. The children looked happy. The staff were nice people." He looked blandly at Macdonald.

The man held his gaze for a moment, then made a note. "Thank you for your time," he said, rising and shaking hands again. "Enjoy your trip and safe voyage home."

"Thanks," said Peter. The younger official opened the door and returned Peter to the corridor where Wu was waiting, a nervous grimace pasted to his face.

"Everything okay?"

"Yup. Let's go register an adoption and get cracking on those immigration papers," said Peter, smiling with what he hoped was confidence.

After they concluded their business, Wu said he had to return to get the Stedmans for their appointment at the consulate. He offered Peter a ride back to the hotel but Peter wasn't in a rush to be back inside, so instead took directions from Wu, then strolled along Nanjing Road until he found the wide, paved path built atop the Huangpu River embankment: the Bund, where he and Annie had walked briefly in the fog earlier that day.

A sea breeze was dispersing the fog and the sun was beginning to burn through. They were walking among the most desirable addresses in Shanghai — if you liked European architecture from the nineteenth and early twentieth centuries. It looked more like Switzerland than China. And it looked expensive. Peter took a few pictures, asked a German tourist to take one of him and Annie together. He tried to put the day's events from his mind.

They returned to eat supper with the Stedmans at a restaurant recommended in a glossy brochure they had picked up at the hotel. It was a short walk away in the opposite direction from the park. They were glad they had ordered several dishes, as the servings were small. Crab, fish with vegetables, meatballs, rice and fried noodles. Everyone tried a bit of everything, the way you do in Chinese restaurants, wherever you might be.

The Stedmans' appointment had gone off all right so they were free to sightsee the next day. They'd arranged with Wu to visit the old city and the Yuyuan Garden. Peter said he'd love to tag along.

He put Annie to bed, then spoke quietly with Jan on the telephone. She was fine, the girls were fine; the weather was delightful. She'd had two police officers at the house and she and they had gone through Eleanor's paperwork. They'd taken the files that seemed sensitive, mainly Eleanor's profiles of dissidents. What was it all about? Was he in danger?

Peter soothed Jan by reminding her he'd be home in six more days.

"I'll contact the police when I get back and see what they make of it. It could be nothing to do with Eleanor's activities. It could be students trying to hack into the university computer system and I was just the unlucky one they picked on." He paused, then casually asked, "Did you make an appointment for Annie with Dr. Stone, like we did for Jenny and Liza? There's a scar I'd like checked...no, no, it's healed. On her abdomen on the right. Yeah, probably appendix or an accident. Oh, and I'll email you the photos I've taken so far. Bye, love. Wish you were here."

No, I don't, he thought, as he prepared for bed. He didn't fall asleep for hours.

The sun was shining clearly on the morning of their second day in Shanghai as a beaming and garrulous Wu escorted the little party into a minivan. Peter observed with amusement that Amanda had dressed Julia in an outfit that matched her own: mother and daughter were wearing yellow jumpsuits, straw sandals and straw sunhats. Then Wu took Peter aside and explained that he had been asked to return to the consulate again today but not until late afternoon. Peter's stomach gave a flip but he pretended nonchalance as he climbed into the van. He wondered if there would be another visit with Macdonald.

"Today we're visiting the Chenghuang Miao district: very old, very nice. You will like it. Beautiful temple where the people of Shanghai remember the gods of the city. Then, if we have time, we will visit the Yuyuan Garden, the Garden of Happiness, the most beautiful garden in China."

Wu chatted away and soon they had arrived at City God Temple. When Peter saw people lighting handfuls of long incense sticks at the large brazier in the temple's courtyard, he felt a disconnect between what he thought of as secular China, that is, Communist China, and the practice of religion, but listening to Wu's explanations understood that the old religions were part of China's cultural heritage and as such could be tolerated and absorbed under the present system of government. City God was a Taoist temple.

After lunch in a nearby noodle house, they walked to the Yuyuan Garden, a place of great beauty, as Wu had said, and of contrast. Some of the buildings were large and flashy with extravagant flared roofs, interspersed with covered bridges and large pools full of fish. Others were modest dwellings where one could imagine a solitary scholar meditating or writing from a position on the porch close to the still water: a clump of succulent-leaved plants would provide a focus for thought.

This beauty, Peter thought. How reconcile it with the damage people do? He thought of Eleanor's dissidents, some disappeared and presumed imprisoned or executed. And thought of Canada's wilderness areas, some spoiled by open-pit mining and extraction, or by hydro electrical development, or endangered by pipelines; the First Nations people struggling with the government for their human rights, for control of the land.

Peter hoped he wasn't naïve. He knew some native Canadians would sell or develop the land to the detriment of its natural beauty. Similarly, he could imagine how difficult governing such an immense and diverse land as China would be; especially as much of the population remembered or had heard their parents speak of famine times.

A squeal from Annie brought him back to his present reality. Each large area of the garden was separated from its neighbours by dragon walls, so called because where the wall ended and opened into the next section, a large stone dragon head was mounted atop the wall, snarling as it guarded the division. Annie's attention had been caught by one such dragon.

Peter and Annie played a game. Every time they approached a dragon, Peter began to point and growl softly. Annie would look for the dragon and, finding it, pretend to be afraid, bury her face in his shoulder or cover her eyes, only to peek out at him and the dragon and laugh.

"You've really got a way with children," said Josh, admiringly.

"I enjoy them," said Peter, giving his daughter a hug. "I really enjoy them."

They had by no means finished seeing all the gardens when Wu said it was time for him and Peter to leave for their next appointment at the Canadian consulate. This time the meeting was straightforward and with the immigration department only. There was no sign of Macdonald and all Peter had to do was sign something that had been forgotten the previous day. Annie's papers were promised for the day before their flight home. Wu dropped an emotionally exhausted Peter off at the hotel and went to rejoin the Stedmans at the garden.

Annie was tired and went to sleep on one of the beds. Peter made tea and sipped it while rereading the journal he'd kept for the trip. He'd meant to use it to list ideas and images for future poems. Instead, it had mostly descended to the level of describing what they had eaten or seen and what Annie was like. He'd self-censored any of the negative impressions but they were fresh in his mind so he abbreviated and jotted them down in the journal in the order in which they had occurred:

1. orph. dir. & nan. tense
2. is A., A?

3. A. sc. ab.

4. off. comp. theft

5. Ch? not gd.

6. where orph. dir? wh. nan?

7. sold. nxt. dr

8. surg. orph?

9. consul? Mac?

Peter hadn't realized there were so many elements contributing to his sense of unease. All of them, taken separately, were small — well, Annie's scar would be important to her personally, but everything else seemed minor. So the director and nanny had seemed tense during the adoption. Maybe they had some personal thing going; the boss/employee relationship was never easy. And Annie being Annie — well, that one they'd never know but he knew that he was happy to adopt her and bring her to Canada into his family. The theft of the office computer could be random; the driver, Chen, simply rude. And what would be more natural than that soldiers stationed next door to an orphanage should run to put out its fire? For all he knew, every orphanage in China had a surgical unit in its basement and he could put his meeting with Mr. Macdonald at the Canadian consulate down to a random spot check. These civil servants had to justify their existences.

It was just that when he sequenced the events and added them up, it seemed that something — not necessarily directly about him or Annie — seemed wrong.

5

As the next few days passed in sightseeing, Peter began to long for his own small town, to get out of Shanghai's pollution, traffic and noise. He found the Pudong New Area with its glittering towers too much. Wu, who was proud of this district, seemed to think the Westerners would enjoy it but there were only so many skyscrapers Peter could crane his neck to look up at before he felt saturated.

The afternoon they spent cruising on the Huangpu River, from the Bund to the mouth of the Yangzi River and back, was a time when he felt he caught his breath, when things slowed down. He remembered how water always had this effect on him: whether in a canoe in Algonquin Park or on a ferry to the Toronto Islands, he found being motionless while floating on water soothing. And to be in transit was a welcome temporary escape from all the details that were jostling in his mind.

Wu met them at the wharf with the good news that the exit papers for both parties were complete. They decided their last day should be a quiet one spent close to the hotel, shopping and packing.

That night, at supper in the hotel, Peter could sense Amanda and Josh retreating from any intimacy with him, distancing themselves against any future contact in Canada, even while they exchanged contact information.

"Next time we're visiting Toronto," said Josh heartily, "we'll have to get together." Peter refrained from reminding him that he didn't live in Toronto but in a small town almost two hours away from that city's centre. He smiled and nodded and made a bet with himself that once back in Canada, he'd never hear from the Stedmans again. It was normal. He didn't take it personally. All they had in common was the fact of their Chinese adoptions, their little girls.

So the next day Peter wasn't surprised when the Stedmans announced they were going to a ritzy shopping district with Wu. They knew he wouldn't be interested. He decided to return to the Garden of Happiness and spend a quiet time revisiting the dragon heads and goldfish with Annie.

As he walked from the hotel to the garden he felt energized and happy. He sang a little five-word song in his head—"The last day in China, The last day in China"—then found himself humming first the tune and then the words out loud to Annie. He knew he'd been homesick but had underestimated how much.

As he strode along the sidewalk he noticed that a race or fun-run was in progress in the street. Runners were coming up quite close behind him before passing. He wondered if the run was to benefit a disease as so many were in Canada. A lot of the T-shirts the runners were wearing were pink but he didn't get why until some girls wearing rainbows on their shirts jogged by smiling and waving to Annie.

A gay pride event in China? He couldn't quite believe the homosexual community would be so daring. It must be legal. He noticed a lot of foreigners among the racers and wondered how many Chinese would be brave enough to come out this way.

Some of the runners carried small bags and were throwing red-wrapped candies at children walking on the sidewalks. Peter caught a couple. He and Annie continued along, enjoying their treats.

Arriving at the garden, he quickly went through the sections they'd already seen and resumed the tour where they'd left off the day before. Annie didn't enjoy the dragon game today, appearing genuinely frightened by the ornate, roaring creatures, but she still liked to look down at the goldfish. They stood on a bridge that appeared to float in small crooked sections across a pond. They passed through a rounded gate — a circle in a wall — and found themselves in a grotto where gnarly, weathered rocks were piled. A dark doorway under a mound appealed for its mystery and they went in.

The sounds of the city of Shanghai, already muffled by the garden's foliage, were further distanced in the little cave and the temperature dropped a few degrees. Peter checked Annie but she didn't seem frightened by the dark and they were having a quiet moment on a stone bench when a small Chinese man entered abruptly.

He was slim with dyed blond hair and was dressed for jogging in white shorts and singlet with blue trim. On one wrist he wore a pale pink and white flat plastic bracelet.

"Your last day in China, I think?" he said with a smile.

Peter was too stupefied to speak. This was one of the first Chinese people (other than shopkeepers or other tourists eager to practise their English) to initiate conversation with him and the man had perfect English.

Peter managed to blurt out, "Did you follow us from the run?" and began to edge toward the cave entrance.

"Please stop. I have something for your daughter." He reached into a pocket and produced a wrapped candy for Annie. He added, "And for you," as he pushed a red USB key into Peter's hand.

Peter rejected it, trying to give it back to the young man, saying, "No, no, I can't," but the fellow simply turned and jogged away.

Peter quickly put the key into a pocket and slowly came out into the sun. He unwrapped Annie's candy for her and looked for a place to sit. Plenty of rocks. He picked one and sank down on it. Suddenly he felt afraid. What if hidden cameras had spotted him, and then the man, entering the cave? What if the man was wanted for something? He calmed down when he realized they'd only been in there for a few seconds, thirty maybe. And he had Annie to lend innocence to his actions.

He walked to the next garden and watched the fish swim through the water there. Golden, silver, they jerked in unison, as if one mind operated them all. He considered dropping the USB into the water but, again, what if there were cameras to observe his actions? Would water damage the USB enough so that its contents could not be retrieved? What could it contain? He felt suddenly as if he was part of the action in a type of book he rarely read. He looked at Annie — such a placid little thing. "Let's get out of here," he said in a determined voice. "Let's just get home."

On the walk back to the hotel Peter ducked into an electronics store and purchased four red USB keys that he thought were identical to the one in his pocket. Safety in numbers, he thought. He also bought an assortment of cables and a cellphone, burbling happily to the clerk as he paid, "Your prices are very good, much cheaper than at home." The clerk nodded, smiling politely.

Back at the hotel Peter made his excuses to the Stedmans and ordered a room service supper. Packing late that night as Annie slept, he first removed the packaging from all of the electronic products and, for good measure, from the souvenirs he'd previously purchased, leaving the plastic wrap and cardboard jumbled together on one of the room's armchairs. Using the knife from his supper plate, he scraped a tiny amount of red paint off of the end of the USB he'd been given before mixing it with the rest. One new USB he returned to his pants pocket. He'd throw it away somewhere far from the hotel the next day.

He decided to just put electronics and souvenirs in with his dirty laundry in one of the big suitcases that would be checked in at the airline counter. He left the suitcase unlocked. If the suspect

USB was detected and examined he would simply produce the bill and act outraged that he'd been sold a used one. And see how far that got him.

Now that he'd figured out how to get the key out of China, he supposed he better take a look and see what was so important about it. What if it contained porn? He'd look an idiot. Already he felt that he was overreacting.

He pushed the USB key into the laptop receptacle. While it downloaded he looked aimlessly around the room, running his plans through his head. He thought he had a good way of disposing of the USB in his pocket. He couldn't throw it away at the hotel or the airport in case he was being watched. Why throw away a perfectly good USB? No, he had to destroy it. He'd set his alarm early by that extra hour he estimated he needed. He'd memorized the Chinese name of the location he needed to visit the next morning. But just to make sure, he had written it out on a piece of paper and put it in his pants pocket.

He clicked on the document and began to read. Someone had been meticulous. Copies of personal files and below each an English translation. Names and places, dates of birth, detention and death, and, chillingly, blood type. So these were medical files? Each entry included an identity photo. As Peter looked more closely at the photos, he realized from the glazed eyes and slack jaws that some had been taken after death. All the photos were of adults and some were labelled Falun Gong, Tibetan, Uighur, Christian.

A slight noise as Annie turned on her bed made him jerk his head up and around. She slept on.

He scrolled down to where a new section of the document began. Lists. One was titled "Kidneys." He clicked.

Information followed tracking single organs as they were moved from donor to recipient. Then another extensive file indicated the provinces from which the organs had come.

In fascinated horror Peter clicked on Fujian province and the next list appeared. The name of the town where Annie's orphanage was located appeared halfway down the list.

Peter rushed into the bathroom retching. He hung his head over the toilet bowl until his stomach had calmed somewhat, flushed the handle, then rose shakily and sat on the toilet lid. He turned toward the sink, splashed water on his face and into his mouth.

He returned to the bedroom and lay on his bed, one forearm raised up to cover his eyes. He purposely breathed slowly a few times. Then he rose, deleted the file, closed the computer and returned the USB to its place, wrapped in a sock in his suitcase.

He got into bed repeating a variation on his mantra — the last night in China, the last night in China — until he fell asleep.

As it turned out, he needn't have set the alarm. Annie woke fretting and crying an hour before they needed to get up and by the time he soothed her back to sleep his going back to bed wasn't worthwhile.

He showered for a long time, then shaved carefully, staring at his weary face. He thought a few more of his remaining brown hairs had certainly turned grey during the trip and that the pouches under his eyes, usually barely visible, were positively bulging. He pressed a cold wet washcloth over them as he lay down waiting for the alarm to ring.

He must have dozed off, as when he woke, he was lying on his side and the washcloth had soaked through the collar of his shirt. The alarm buzzed and he woke Annie gently, gave her some juice to drink and carefully put her in the sling.

"Here's a cookie, sweetie," he said. "We just have to go for a little ride."

He stuck his head cautiously out the hotel room door, half expecting some lurking menace to pounce. Nothing. Of course.

No one except the young runner knew Peter had the USB key and the information. It's all in your head, Peter told himself as he straightened and walked to the elevator. Nothing to be afraid of, he thought, as they descended. Nobody watching you, as they left the elevator, crossed the lobby and got into a cab.

He said the name City God Temple first in English and then carefully pronounced it in Chinese before wrapping the address paper around the new USB and returning the package to his pocket. He felt the taxi driver's eyes returning to the rear-view mirror time and again, checking to see what else Peter or Annie might do.

When they arrived Peter decided not to have the taxi wait. He'd take his chances finding another one. He walked into the courtyard of the temple and let his breath out in relief. Thank God or the gods that even this early the temple gates were open and the coals in the large brazier, the size of a wide coffin, were burning.

He gave some money to one of the priests, a man about his own age, he judged, and was handed a thick bunch of incense sticks. Peter took them with his left hand while he removed the paper-wrapped USB from his pocket with his right.

The day they'd visited he'd observed that while some people took their lit incense away from the fire and carried it as they visited the temple, it was not unusual for others to stand in front of the brazier for as long as it took to burn their incense. He needed to do the latter.

Transferring the incense to his right hand, he lowered it onto the glowing coals, at the same time dropping the USB into the brazier as close to the side nearest him as he could. Holding Annie in her sling to one side, he then turned the incense so the lit ends were facing him and used them to push the package down and under some coals. He withdrew the flaming and half-burnt incense from the fire and blew on it to make smoke. He closed his eyes and stepped back from the heat of the brazier, caught a whiff of burning plastic. Panicked, he waved his incense in different directions. Its fragrance soon overpowered the other smell and he was left with a handful of slender sticks to drop into the brazier.

"Mission accomplished," he said to Annie. He might be paranoid — heck, he *was* paranoid — but at least the number of USBs in his luggage matched the number on the invoice from the store. What he'd doubted water could destroy had surely been destroyed by fire. He hoped the gods of Shanghai would be with them today.

Back at the hotel he saw the Stedmans and Wu standing in the lobby. Wu's normally smiling face changed from worried to happy when he spotted Peter.

"Oh, Mr. Forrest, I thought I had lost you!" he exclaimed, his lips stretching wide. A bubble of spit clung to one corner of his mouth. "It's almost time to leave."

"Just went for a last look around," said Peter affably. "Probably won't ever be back in Shanghai."

Wu accompanied Peter to the room to fetch the luggage. Peter gave him the envelope of cash he'd prepared the night before.

"Thank you for all your help, Wu. You were a very pleasant guide to us."

"You are most welcome," said a delighted Wu. "And Annie is fortunate I think to have such a father."

There was relative silence during the ride to the airport, except to point out sites they'd either seen or wished they'd had time to see. It had been an exhilarating and exhausting trip for the Stedmans, as new parents, and one of mounting tension for the veteran, Peter.

Wu helped them get baggage carts and print their boarding passes, then watched as they joined the lines to check in. Peter glimpsed another man had joined Wu and the two were quietly discussing something.

Peter had all the necessary documents zipped into the pockets of his travel pants. He had Annie in her sling, her diaper bag slung over his other shoulder and his laptop in its case as carry-on luggage. When it was his turn he put the diaper bag and computer case on the floor between his feet and hoisted first one and then the other of their two large suitcases onto the conveyor belt. He wondered if those large suitcases were off to be x-rayed and whether computer keys, cables and a cellphone could be considered homemade bomb materials. As he waited for the airline clerk to check his boarding pass, he comforted himself with the thought that even if someone opened his bag they would find the electronics casually among his socks and underwear and, somewhere in there, the itemized bill from the electronics store.

The suitcases disappeared into the wall behind the desk. On to security. The long shuffle as the line snaked back and forth. The emptying of the pockets and removal of shoes. Even Annie's tiny slippers were placed in one of the plastic tubs along with the sling. They walked through the metal detector together. No alarms went off. No red lights flashed. The scan was likewise negative. Then the pat down. They were through.

Peter slipped on his shoes and gathered his child and bags into his arms. As always, he first found his departure gate, then bought a large coffee, a carton of milk for Annie and two pastries. Two hours until boarding could commence.

The Stedmans appeared and settled nearby. Amanda said she was going to look around in the shops. Josh also bought some snacks and he and Peter sat sipping their coffees while feeding the babies torn-off bits of pastry. Josh seemed as burnt out as Peter.

Peter grinned and leaned over. "It gets better," he said, "and then it gets worse and better and worse —"

"I get it," said Josh and, as Julia flung herself backwards with a roar, added, "patience, Daddy, patience."

The two hours' wait until the boarding call stretched into three. A flight delay was announced. Peter took Annie for little walks while Josh watched his stuff, then Peter returned the favour.

He bought and drank another coffee. He changed Annie's diaper in an airport toilet. He knew changing her on the plane would be tricky and hoped only to have to do it once or twice.

Finally the pre-boarding was announced. As Peter joined the Stedmans and a few other families with small children going to the head of the line, he saw the man he'd seen talking to Wu sitting across from their flight's waiting area and, at first, thought it was his driver, Chen, from the orphanage visit. The man was dressed similarly in grey pants and long-sleeved white shirt except this man was thinner. Peter felt the sweat trickle down the back of his neck as the clerk checked his and Annie's boarding passes and passports and then they were walking down the passageway to their plane. They found their seats, the other passengers boarded; they waited as the luggage was loaded into the belly of the plane. Surely, thought Peter, they would have called me by now if they'd found anything suspicious in the suitcases. As the plane taxied and took off he leaned back in his seat, felt all his muscles loosen and prepared to enjoy the ride.

Passing through Canadian customs was a breeze. Peter had nothing to hide from them. Cheerfully, if tiredly, he itemized all the souvenirs he'd purchased. He was quickly processed, the luggage appeared without delay, and he was able to identify his bags, thanks to the red and white wool tied to their handles. He saw Jan and the girls, all wearing summer dresses and looking happy and excited.

As he leaned in to kiss Jan and smelled her freshly shampooed hair, she quipped, "Welcome to yesterday. Or is it tomorrow? I can never remember."

"It's tomorrow," he replied and then he cried.

6

"Daddy's just tired," Jan reassured a horrified Jenny and Liza. She took Annie out of the sling and transferred the baby into the double stroller she'd brought. She put Liza into the seat in front. "Jenny, I need you to hold on to Daddy's hand. Come on, everybody. Who wants a doughnut?" She turned to Peter. "We'll grab a meal along the way, okay, dear?"

Peter blew his nose and shakily said, "It's just so good to be home, everyone. It's so good to see you all." He smiled, resuming his normal tones. "I brought presents for when we get home." Jenny threw herself at his legs, clasping them and begging to know what her present was. "Lunch first, then presents," he promised, putting his arm around Jan as they walked to the car. "Lots to tell you," he said.

"Lots to tell you too," she smiled and squeezed him around the waist.

Heading east on the 401, it wasn't long before they were clear of Toronto. Jan stopped at the first rest stop, which featured the DeWitt-Forrest family's favourite food: soup and sandwiches, doughnuts and coffee.

While Jan made the order with the two older girls hopping around her calling out food suggestions, Peter sat at a table with Annie. He kept taking deep breaths and sighing them out. He took Annie out of the stroller and sat her on his lap. When the food arrived he said, "Your first doughnut hole, Annie. Now you're really Canadian."

As they continued their drive home after lunch, he held Jan's hand and looked out at the rolling hills and forested valleys, the pasture land, the emptiness.

"Where are all the people?" he muttered.

"What?"

"The people. There aren't any except in cars on the road and in the odd house here and there. Why is that? Why live in a city when you could live here?"

"Most people don't have your appetite for long-distance driving," Jan teased. She looked briefly in the rear-view mirror. "They seem to be getting along."

Liza was sleeping, as she usually did in the car, but Jenny was passing Annie an assortment of objects from the kids' activity box they kept in the back seat and offering her assessment of each as she did. True, she wasn't letting Annie retain possession of any one object for very long, but that was Jenny.

After a brief look back, Peter straightened, then felt himself nodding off, his head slipping to one side. He awoke as they left the highway, turned south and headed for Dunbarton, passing the gas station and a large fruit and vegetable market.

He vaguely heard the inevitable request made by Jenny every time they passed the petting zoo. "Can we stop and see the animals? I want to see the bunnies. Can we?" In her short life Jenny had already learned that persistence pays dividends.

"Not today, honey. Daddy and Annie need to sleep. Maybe tomorrow." Jan turned to look at Peter. "Can't keep them open, eh?"

"Oh, sorry. What? No, I need my bed. Maybe two hours then wake me up. I don't want to get too turned around. And I want to hear all your news."

On a road off a road off a road was how Peter described the location of their home to visitors. The long driveway was gravel, most of which had eroded to reveal the packed earth of the original farm track. Flanked by fenced meadows on either side, it led to the house, protected on the north, west and east sides by mature trees, and flaunting ornamental shrubs like lilac and mock orange to the south. The house itself was a two-storey square box with a flat lid, made of the local grey granite, the trim painted white.

Jan turned left into the circular driveway and parked. "Which bag are the presents in?" she asked.

"The blue one," Peter replied, "and thank you."

"For what?"

"For your sensitive observation that if I don't get to bed right now, I will be tempted to fall asleep right here in the car or melt from exhaustion."

He staggered through the front door of the house and straight upstairs, threw off his clothes and closed his eyes.

He was in bed with Eleanor in the bedroom of her old Toronto apartment. The window was open and, because there are few mosquitoes in Toronto, unscreened, so sunlight, breeze and the distant hum of the city could enter the room unimpeded. The walls were pale blue and the bed coverlet was green. Chinese prints hung on the walls, mostly scenes of placid nature — a waterfall, a hermit climbing a mountain path — but one depicted a struggle between two forces: a tiger perched high on a mountain crag snarled and raised one clawing paw as a screaming eagle descended towards it, wings and talons outstretched.

He was young and Eleanor was young too, younger than she'd ever been when he'd known her. She caressed him, mounted him, and rocked gently forward and back, forward and back.

"Daddy, who gets the jewellery boxes?" Jenny's high voice pierced his dream and he opened his eyes to look directly into hers. She held one of the boxes, the paper umbrella and assorted bamboo carvings, and she was pushing rhythmically against the bed with her body.

"You and Liza get the jewellery boxes," he said, pulling on his shorts under the covers, then swinging his legs over the side of the bed. "Mummy gets the umbrella, if she wants it, and you girls share everything else. The cables and things are for me. Put them back in my suitcase, okay?"

"Why didn't you buy a jewellery box for Annie?"

"You're right, why didn't I? I guess I was thinking a little baby doesn't need one. Not like you big girls." This worked: Jenny preened herself, straightened with pride.

Jan stuck her head into the room. "Jenny, I told you to leave your father alone."

"I'm going for a shower," said Peter, standing and stretching.

Relaxing under the hot stream of water, he looked out the window. After hotel rooms for two weeks, it was a luxury to have a bathroom with a window. The fresh June foliage was restful to look at. He wondered if Jan had mowed the lawn recently.

The day passed in the delightful normalcy of a family at home together. Jan hung the umbrella in a high corner of the living room where its reds and blues on a gold background made a rich accent note. Peter gathered the electronics from among his dirty clothes, put them in a drawer of the television stand and did a load of laundry. He inspected but did not cut the overlong grass. Tomorrow.

Supper was spaghetti, garlic bread, salad and red wine, and all the carbs, combined with jetlag, made him pass out on the sofa afterwards. He woke up when the television went on and Jan sat next to him, putting his feet on her lap and resting her own on the coffee table. "So?" she asked.

"You first."

She brought him up to speed with news of Jenny's preschool's end-of-year party — at the park, good cake — and Liza's cutting two more baby teeth. The peas were flowering and she, Jan, had planted more beans where the first planting had failed or had been eaten by rabbits. The guy who was going to remodel the downstairs bathroom had called; he'd be available in August not July. She'd made an appointment for Annie with Dr. Stone. No one from the police had contacted her since she'd handed over Eleanor's notes and files.

"So that should be that," she concluded.

"Mmm."

"What does 'mmm' mean?"

"It means something — some weird things — happened in China. A guy gave me a USB key and then just took off. When I looked at the contents it seemed to be information about the organization of organ harvesting — on a national level — from prisoners."

"Do you think it's a leak?"

"I don't know. I was so distracted by the material I really didn't consider the guy himself. Anyway — "

"Anyway, you risked everything just to smuggle something out of China?" Jan's voice contained a rising note of disbelief that made Peter remove his feet from her lap and sit up.

"Jan, Jan, Annie's town was on the list of places where organs are harvested or transplanted. There was a team of surgeons operating in the basement when I was there. After I saw her scar, I didn't know what to think. That's why I want Dr. Stone to check her out to see if something is missing. Other kids, Jan, it might be happening to other kids. It might be the organized harvesting of organs from children, from orphans."

"That's horrible. Okay, I get it. Her appointment is next week. First we do that. Second, you get rid of that USB to the police or to Amnesty International — I don't care — just get it away from our children."

"I will. Of course I will. Do you think I asked for any of this to happen?"

"No, I know you didn't." Jan leaned over and rested her head against his.

He kissed her. So soft, her lips. "Bed?"

"Bed." She pressed close. "I've missed you, Peter."

Jan had an early exercise class and was gone by the time Peter and the girls awoke the next morning. They had a leisurely breakfast, then he dressed the two youngest while Jenny tried on an assortment of clothes before she found the right combination for her day. He was just loading the dishwasher when Jan returned, glowing from her workout.

"Well, you look all bright-eyed and bushy-tailed!"

"Thanks. Do people still say that? And you a poet. Wish I could say the same about you."

"I just need a few days' downtime. And more beauty sleep. I'm going to do a little work on Eleanor's poems now, then this aft I want to cut the lawn."

"Yes, well, about the lawn, sorry. I left it too long and then, when I tried to cut it…"

"It's fine, hon, it's just the sort of chore I love. So poetry, lunch, lawn."

"All right. I'll see you at lunch."

Peter happily retreated to the back room behind the kitchen and closed the door to block out the sound of the dishwasher. He retrieved his laptop and Eleanor's paper files of poems and sat on the brown leather sofa where he did most of his work. Soon he was surrounded with poems and notes laid out on the sofa and the floor at his feet.

Eleanor had divided the manuscript into four sections. The first contained short poems, some cryptic, some deceptively clear. One in particular, the first one, which could certainly title the section or even the whole book, was called "The Key." Peter absorbed the graphic imagery of the language and intuited its meaning: that effort towards any successful endeavour was necessary, painful and repetitive. "One Daisy" referred to the value of the individual as separate from the collective. And "Strange" was one of those poems that hooked from line to line, the previous line's meaning changing as the next line's became apparent until the end, at which point the reader returned to the beginning to retrace the poet's thinking.

Peter liked this section of the book very much and put it aside. All it needed was a possible reordering of the poems. The next section began a descent into a hell where calm belief in the rights of the individual led to the butchery of said individual. An image of bodies laid out in rows, their decapitated heads piled separately. Another of anguished dead discoloured faces twisted to one side above bodies that displayed either gaping cavities or black, stitched scars.

Eleanor's notes for these poems mentioned something called Falun Gong and referenced photos she'd seen on the Internet. In dread, Peter opened his laptop and saw what had inspired these poems. He closed the laptop and looked out through the full-length sliding glass doors where Jan was hanging laundry as the kids played in the pile of sand that somehow had never become a sandbox. The sheer white curtains embroidered with stars moved in time to the irregular small wafts of summer breeze.

He realized he was face to face with something he'd always avoided: the difficulties of others not personally known to him. Sure, he had his charities: the War Amps who provided child amputees with limbs and activities were his favourite. He even volunteered and sat on the district's Senior Advocacy Board, making sure seniors were able to access the services to which they were entitled. "Twisting the government's arm," he and Jan called it. And he sent money to special appeals after storms and earthquakes.

But the persecution of Falun Gong in China was different. It meant the sustained detention, torture and death of millions (millions!) of people who happened to belong to — what? — a cult that practised meditation and other spiritual exercises. And demanded the right to do so.

A movement that incorporated mostly Buddhist precepts — truthfulness, compassion (ah, Eleanor, he thought), forbearance — but also some Taoist and Confucian traditions and which by the late 1990s had numbered its adherents in the tens of millions. Some of them had demonstrated peacefully in 1999 in Beijing, requesting legal recognition and freedom from the state. Previous to that time, the Chinese government had seemed to support the Falun Gong but after the Beijing demonstration policy shifted and it was declared a "heretical organization." Since that policy change, Falun Gong members had been harassed, imprisoned, forced to labour in factories and were subject to torture and execution. A 2006 Canadian study linked the execution of Falun Gong members to organ harvesting and the international organ market.

Despite this persecution, many Chinese still continued to practise the Falun Gong meditative and physical exercises, giving up smoking, drinking, drug use, and nonmarital or homosexual sex.

The reasons for the Chinese government ban of Falun Gong were many: it seemed to Peter to boil down to noncompliance with Communist Party ideology and the fact that it was so popular it might prove a threat to the party's hegemony. The spiritual component reminded him of the self-immolation of Tibetan monks and dissidents — a similarity that would not have escaped the Chinese government. He looked down at the side table where the clock that had been his mother's — a whimsical blue porcelain apple with the clock face embedded in one side — told him it was time for lunch. He picked it up and turned it over. Made in China.

In the kitchen he lined up bread, ham, cheese, mayo and mustard on the counter and began building sandwiches. Four should be enough. He boiled water and made a couple of instant noodle soups. The kids loved to slurp noodles.

"Yay, Daddy made lunch," said Jan as the gang poured in. "Annie's been walking and playing all morning. She's going to sleep well this afternoon."

"But we're going to see bunnies," protested Jenny.

"That can still happen," replied Peter. "Annie sleeps, I cut grass, you guys visit bunnies. Feed some for me, okay?"

Peter waved as Jan and the girls left for the petting zoo, then got out the rake and wheelbarrow. Before he could cut the rough mess Jan had left him, he needed to remove the rotting cut grass that lay in clumps on the lawn. For an hour he thought of nothing else. He checked Annie. Still asleep in her crib. He touched her head and covered her with the thin summer blanket. Then he cut the lawn.

He was having a well-deserved beer on the porch when a white Crown Victoria drove up. Two men got out and showed him their identification. Toronto police. Detective Sergeant Robert Smith and Detective Douglas Smythe. The same two who had visited Jan while he was away. They were both tall men, well groomed. Peter immediately thought of the detectives Thomson and Thompson in his beloved Tintin books (he had them all) and his lips curved slightly.

"Yeah, hilarious us having similar names," said a straight-faced Smith. He was blond and blue-eyed and, on closer inspection, a bit heavier than his partner.

Peter straightened. "Not at all, officer. Probably frustrating for you and your partner. Confusion and so on. Come in." The officers seated themselves in the living room. Peter asked, "Is this about my office break-in?"

"Perhaps. We'd like to know more about your relationship with Eleanor Brandon. When did you last see or have contact with the deceased?"

"Eleanor?" Peter was surprised and showed it. "Well, we kept in touch by email, but the last time I saw her was at a book awards dinner, oh, it must have been last fall, so about six or seven months ago."

"And how was Ms. Brandon at that time?"

"Fine, fine. We talked. She mostly about her work and writing and me about my family." Peter smiled, gesturing at the litter of toys on the floor of the living room. "We have three little girls."

"And you've just recently returned from China." Smythe spoke in similar tones to Smith: serious, impersonal. "You adopted your third child."

"Well, you know that," Peter said easily. Of the two, Smythe seemed the more subtle, a bit harder to read than Smith. His hair was light brown, his eyes hazel. He had a small blue notebook and a pen resting on his knee.

Back to Smith. "And how was that adoption, sir? Similar to the first two?"

"Yes, except it was from Shanghai instead of Beijing, as the first two had been." He hesitated. "Do you want to know if anything odd happened at any time while I was in China?"

"That might be helpful, sir." Smythe leaned forward in his chair. "I'll be taking notes, so take your time."

Peter thought to himself, what is it about police? Even when you're innocent, you feel uncomfortable.

"After the adoption, I visited the orphanage where my daughter, Annie, had been living. To take pictures so we could give her a sense of her place of origin when she's older." He paused and Smythe interjected, "And they were okay with you taking pictures?"

"They said just the outside of the building, the gardens. No shots of rooms or kids. Understandably. The privacy of the children."

"Oh, completely understandable, sir, from their point of view. But you did see the inside of the facility?"

Smith was listening to this exchange, gazing around the room, studying Peter, then looking out the window. If a policeman could be said to fidget, he was fidgeting.

Peter decided to speak. "Is something wrong, officer?"

Smith gave Peter a dirty look, then tried to relax on the couch where he was sitting. "No, no. Carry on."

"We walked to the top of the building — fine view of the city and the forest behind — and I took pictures, and then we toured the building, going down floor by floor, until a fire alarm went off when we were on the second floor, I think, and we left." Peter recounted seeing the surgical team, how the soldiers from next door had arrived before any firefighters made an appearance, how the fire had seemed small and easily contained, and his departure.

Smythe interjected. "Any objections to us having a look at those photographs, Mr. Forrest?"

"None at all. I'll email them to you. But what has this got to do with Eleanor's death?" Peter felt he should have asked this question earlier.

Smith glared then spoke. "It's possible it wasn't suicide. Coroner may have jumped the gun due to the combination of deceased's known membership in right-to-die organizations and her doctor's diagnosis."

"I never heard…" Peter trailed off.

Smythe referred to his notes. "Stage four ovarian cancer." He looked up. "I thought there were five stages of cancer before you die."

"Ovarian cancer only goes to stage four," Peter replied. "Eleanor would have known that, because the same disease killed her mother. The last recurrence took place over four years. It was a gruelling experience for Eleanor and her family."

"So when was that, sir?" Smythe was poised to write.

"About twenty years ago, when I was close to Eleanor. She was my teacher and my friend. She was close to her mother and grieved for her for a long time."

"Did you notice anything when you visited her apartment after her death? You had been there before, right?"

Peter turned his attention to Smith. "We were lovers for a short time, so I knew the place, yes. But I can't say I noticed anything in particular." Peter paused in thought. "No, that's not true. I remember thinking it odd that there were no scissors in the kitchen. Eventually I found a small pair on the desk."

"We found the kitchen scissors in the backyard, under her window." Smith's eyes sharpened.

"Well, that's where you'd throw them if you didn't want to be tempted to cut the bag off. Oh…" A light dawned in Peter's eyes. "Right. Why didn't she also throw the little scissors out the window?"

Smith added, "And her tea, her last cup of tea, wasn't finished, wasn't even tasted, apparently. She put the teabag in the compost bucket, added milk and sugar, and then didn't drink it."

"She was interrupted," mused Peter, "by something or someone."

"Did you telephone Ms. Brandon on the day of her death?"

"Telephone?" Peter was surprised. "Oh, yes, the neighbour mentioned she heard Eleanor's phone ring. No. I told you, when we communicated it would most probably just be a casual email to see how the other one was. Our relationship had become — distant."

"So what else happened in China, sir?" Smythe hitched his chair another little bit forward.

"Hmm?" Peter thought he'd heard a sound from upstairs where Annie was sleeping, then changed his mind. His energy sagged as jetlag kicked in again. "Would you guys like some tea or coffee?"

Smith cheered up a bit. "Yeah. Coffee would be great." Smythe nodded.

Peter was relieved to be alone in the kitchen. Eleanor not a suicide? Eleanor murdered? He found some biscuits and added them to the tray with the cream and sugar, then angrily removed them. It's not a bloody tea party, he thought. They're interrogating me. Calm down, an inner voice cautioned. Tell them everything. He put the plate of biscuits back onto the tray, made three instant espressos and returned to the living room. As the officers helped themselves, he went to the television stand and opened a drawer. After lifting several Disney DVDs out of the way, he found and handed the USB key with the little scratch on its paint to Smith.

"I'm just going to get my laptop," he called over his shoulder and retrieved it from the study.

"That" — he pointed to the key—"was given me in China by a man literally off the street." Peter and Smythe joined Smith on the couch as he scrolled through the document to its end.

There was a pause as the men drank their coffee.

Smythe spoke first. "Any comments, Mr. Forrest?"

Peter thought. "Well, it seems to have a bearing on the activism Eleanor was lately working on. And some of her material was among that taken when my office at the university was broken into. But how could that have been connected to her death?"

Smythe was writing. "This is a receipt for the key. Would you recognize the man who gave it to you again? We have pictures we'd like you to look at. When would be convenient?"

It crossed Peter's mind to ask how Toronto police could possibly have a photo of what he presumed was a Chinese dissident. He leaned his elbows on his knees and pressed the heels of his palms into his eyes. The warmth was soothing.

"It's all a bit much," he muttered. "There's Eleanor's death. There are her files on Chinese dissidents. There's my office break-in and theft of my computer there. Annie's orphanage. The USB key. Did I mention I was questioned by what I presume was a security advisor at the Canadian consulate in Shanghai? About my trip to the orphanage."

"We know about that," said Smythe, "and we'll be sharing information with the appropriate agency."

"Oh. Just why is Eleanor's death really being considered suspicious? It's not because of a pair of scissors on her desk."

"Thumbs up," replied Smith.

Numbly, Peter repeated, "Thumbs up."

"If Ms. Brandon struggled to remove the plastic bag taped over her head, changed her mind about her suicide, her thumb prints would have probably been at the same level or lower than her fingerprints." Smith grasped his own neck, loosely. Sure enough, his fingers encircled his jaw near his ears while his thumbs were much lower and met in front near his Adam's apple. "Also, the bag would have been easy enough to tear. The plastic is thin. The markings on her neck indicated the thumbs were up, higher than the other fingers and in front, under her chin." He held his hands out in front of him in the air and mimed their action to suit his words. "Consistent with strangulation by a person unknown." His hands dropped to his sides. "Any more coffee?"

Peter replied, "It was instant." Smith's shoulders slumped, his disappointment visible. "But who would want to murder Eleanor? I can't imagine she had much money and the only person who benefits is her daughter." He got up from the sofa and faced the policemen. "You've seen Dot, I mean Dorothy. She's a small woman like her mother was, and somewhat nervous. She couldn't have…"

"We really have few leads right now and are only suggesting the death is suspicious." Smith put down his empty coffee cup with a sad frown and stood. "We'll be in touch about you viewing photographs, Mr. Forrest. And we may have questions for you regarding the photos you took in China. Thank you for the coffee."

As Smith went down the steps, Smythe murmured in an aside to Peter, "Don't let him bother you. He's trying to quit smoking. Difficult for all of us."

The police car was barely out of his sight when the family car pulled into the driveway.

"I saw who that was. What did they want?" asked Jan.

"Tell you in a bit," said Peter lightly.

"Daddy, we petted llamas," shrieked Jenny. "They have long necks. Like this." And she stretched her neck and bulged her eyes. Peter's tension melted as he joined the family in laughter.

7

"Jenny, you get off of there right now!" Jan matched the words to her action, removing Jenny from the low toy, book and magazine table in the waiting area of Dunbarton's little medical centre and seating her firmly next to her. "Here's a book. Now shush."

Jenny squirmed and wiggled but subsided — for a time. The whole family was dispersed throughout the waiting room. Liza and Annie were engrossed handling parts of a train set, trying to snap bits of track together.

Peter leaned over to Jan. "Still think this was a good idea?" Jan had suggested they all accompany Annie to her first doctor's visit and go on from there to introduce the baby to Jan's mother at her home in a nearby town.

"I didn't say it would be easy," she replied ruefully and made a face.

The receptionist called Annie's name and Peter took her in to meet Dr. Stone, a small, worn-looking woman about ten years his senior. She smiled at Annie and asked Peter several questions about the child's behaviour and health. When it was time for the physical, Dr. Stone switched on the considerable charm she reserved for children.

"Well, hello," she breathed gently, taking the baby slowly from Peter's lap into her arms. "How are you, Annie?" She showed Annie her light then shone it briefly into each eye, ear and into the mouth, all the while speaking softly and moving slowly. "Do you think you could get her shirt open for me?" she asked Peter, warming her stethoscope in her hand before listening to heart and lungs. She palpated the abdomen. Then a quick check of the diaper area and genitals, a few little taps for reflexes and they were done.

Peter waited as she made notes, then spoke. "What about the scar?"

"Were you told anything by the orphanage?"

"I found it the first time I changed her diaper."

"And what did you think?"

"I thought she'd had her appendix out, most likely."

"Ye-es." She paused, writing. "I'm going to order a quick scan at the local hospital so we can find out."

"Oh, do you think it's necessary?"

"The scar is a bit high for an appendectomy."

"Is it?"

"It may just be a different procedure to what I'm used to seeing."

"Yes."

"But I'd like to be sure. And of course there's the other scar."

Peter replied in a daze, "The other scar?"

"Yes. Didn't you notice it? On the other side of the abdomen and very faint. Otherwise," and here Dr. Stone's voice became soft again as she focused on Annie, "otherwise she's a perfect little girl." Her voice normalized. "And you're doing a great job with the diaper area. No rash, no redness even. Keep it up."

Peter decided to take Annie for the scan that day.

"Your mum will have to see her another time," he told Jan. "I want to know. Don't you?"

"Of course. I just hope you don't have to wait too long. Call me when you're done and we'll pick you up." She dropped them at the hospital and went on to her mother's.

Peter assessed the waiting room. There were about six patients already there and more, no doubt, behind the emergency department's sliding doors. So with luck maybe a three-hour wait? He settled in.

He'd brought a book with him, for the wait at Dr. Stone's, but now, as indeed then, he couldn't get into it. Instead his thoughts turned to Eleanor and what her last moments might have been like. If someone had murdered her. He remembered the ancient Greek proverb: "Until he is dead, do not yet call a man happy, but only lucky."

Fortunately Annie continued in her placid behaviour, content to sit on his lap. He shuddered at the thought of waiting this long with the volatile Jenny. He closed his eyes and remembered the first time he and Eleanor had become lovers: his awkwardness as her older body was revealed, her giggles, their mutual relief when they'd finished. He smiled as he remembered that they'd improved with practice. The thought of that body, old, being subjected to violence, was sickening. Annie's name was called and they went through.

Annie giggled when the cold jelly was squirted on her abdomen and her eyes followed the motion of the wand there before turning to look at the ultrasound's lit-up screen.

Peter soon realized that the good thing about an ultrasound, as opposed to an X-ray, was that the technician answered questions about what they were seeing. Of course, she said, it would still have to be confirmed by the doctor, but it appeared that Annie had a normal appendix and one healthy kidney.

Peter held his emotions in check until he was outside the hospital on the phone with Jan.

"One kidney. Probably our child, the real Annie, died, and this one was substituted. Maybe they would have eventually taken the second kidney if we hadn't adopted her." His voice choked. "I knew something was fishy with that orphanage director during the adoption and then she was nowhere to be seen when I visited the orphanage later."

"Peter, calm down. We have her. One kidney is fine." The words were reassuring, but Peter heard the tremble in her voice and wondered if she was reminded of her own anomaly: one ovary absent, one underdeveloped. "We just have to be glad she's with us now. We're coming to get you."

"I'm ravenous. We'll be across the street at the restaurant."

It was late afternoon and the only place within walking distance was a fast food restaurant where Peter would never normally eat. He ordered a chicken burger for him and a small plain burger for Annie. They shared a small order of fries. He ate quickly and the meal first stuck in his throat, then lodged in the centre of his chest.

Jenny was furious when she realized Annie had had an extra treat denied to her and complained all the way home. The usually patient Peter soon had enough and sent her to the room she shared with Liza, where she melted down into a full tantrum, throwing toys and other objects around and screaming the house down.

Liza and Annie, picking up on the emotions of their sister, began crying as well in a concentrated effort to drive their parents crazy.

"Right," said Peter, and mounted the stairs. He opened the door and picked her up. "The other two need to sleep," he said to Jan as he went out the front door, Jenny struggling in his arms. "We're going for a walk."

He put Jenny down on the grass next to the driveway and started walking away from the house.

"No, Daddy, wait," sobbed Jenny, running after him. Together they walked the length of the driveway as her sobs subsided into hiccups. He lifted her so she could check the mailbox. A few flyers. He carried her back to the house and felt her fall asleep, her hands clasped around his neck. Carefully, he put her to bed.

"What was that all about?" asked Jan rhetorically as they collapsed together on the living room sofa. They both had experienced enough of Jenny's tantrums not to take them to heart.

The house quietened. The children were sleeping. Peter said, "I'm angry too. I wish a tantrum would make it go away. What can we do?"

"We can research living with one kidney and help give Annie a great life."

"And the others? The ones in China?"

"Have you contacted Amnesty yet? Or Human Rights Watch? Or both? They'll focus your energies or at least answer your questions. But was Eleanor mixed up in something to do with organ harvesting in China and that was what got her killed? I'm worried for you, Peter. If anything happens to you…"

"You'll raise three delightful children. But nothing is…going to happen to me. Have you eaten? No?" Peter struggled to his feet. "Allow me to microwave Madame some dinner. And let's crack a bottle of wine. We deserve it."

When, the next morning, Peter put the phone down, what stayed with him the longest was the tone of resignation in the voice of the agency representative, as though the man had heard Peter's questions and indignation before. Maybe he, the man, was weary of confirming the same atrocities over and over.

Yes, organ harvesting from prisoners in China was confirmed. Yes, members of Falun Gong were confirmed at risk. And, yes, it was suspected that orphans at some orphanages, especially the sick or disabled, were starved and otherwise neglected until they died and their organs could be harvested. The army, courts, hospitals and police were implicated. Yes, he would be happy to add Peter to their membership. Would Peter want to be made aware of calls to action specifically as related to China or the world? Yes to China. All human rights violations or just pertaining to the Falun Gong or more specifically to forced organ donations?

Peter gulped at the enormity of the problem but fortunately remembered Eleanor's watching brief.

"I'd like to try to continue the work of the poet Eleanor Brandon," he replied. "She was watching over dissidents, especially poets and writers who were in difficulty." Watching over. I like that, he thought. It describes Eleanor's attitude to others. She was watching over someone or many and maybe someone else didn't like that. But killing her? It seemed too far-fetched.

The representative continued. "I'll put you in touch with, or rather, they'll get in touch with you. There's a group that works with Chinese information, tries to verify, contact people there. And thank you for calling."

Peter walked from the study into the kitchen. The house was empty. Jan had headed off to her mother's to introduce Annie. Peter had stayed home, ostensibly to work but, really, he suspected, to think. He felt restless after the phone call, as though he couldn't wait to be doing something, and went for a drive.

Dunbarton was one of the many small to medium towns that occupied the narrow strip of land between Highway 401 to the north and Lake Ontario to the south, so most local drives occurred by default along the east-west corridor. Peter headed east along what used to be the old King's Highway, Route 2, a two-hundred-year-old road that originally stretched from Windsor to Halifax but was now broken up into small roads individually named by their counties.

Peter liked to think of the history of the road: first creeping eastward from Toronto, or York as it was then — a fairly passable road, according to its users, except in late spring and early summer when it became a quagmire no wagon or cart could wallow through. For reasons of accessibility it had paralleled the lake, first complementing river trade then, along with the railroad, supplanting it.

He contrasted his lot with that of the people who settled along the new road back then, pushing settlement further into the bush, farming the land — some flat and fertile, some rocky and sparse — and was thankful for his car and all the labour-saving devices in his house.

After passing through Dunbarton proper with its pharmacy, grocery store, community centre, school, two churches, town hall and half a dozen small shops, his route took him through slight hills where apple orchards and pastures were interrupted by fruit and vegetable markets as well as camping supply stores with stacks of wood, bags of kindling and tanks of propane. Dunbarton was perched between two provincial parks, popular with Torontonians looking for a weekend escape or tourists from farther regions spending their summer vacations. He pulled into Presqu'ile Provincial Park, paid the day user's fee and parked.

It was peak season, almost, and the park was full of people yet large enough for Peter to find solitude after meandering first by the beach and then along a narrow forest trail. He sat on a boulder with a sigh and reached for his notebook and pen.

The poem, when it came, was at first tentative. Annie was there, and anger and resignation, and ghosts were there too — nameless ones with Chinese faces — and Eleanor. And there was shame.

No wonder Eleanor and I rarely talked, he thought. I didn't want to know about the thing most important to her: her fight for justice for those silenced by intimidation, imprisonment and death. "My head up my ass, as usual," he muttered aloud, just as an attractive young woman jogged along the trail near his seat. She gave him a startled look.

Her white shorts and top made him think of the young blond man in China who had given him what he considered important information, doubtless at great personal risk to himself. Was he a member of Falun Gong or a dissident reporter? How on earth had he managed to get such a comprehensive file? Was it from one source or compiled from many? Had he known Eleanor? At least as a friendly foreign contact, if not in person?

Peter turned the page and jotted down who would benefit from Eleanor's death. Dot, charities. He, himself, would only claim expenses from her estate but he supposed he could be considered a suspect. Chinese agents in Canada? Someone in Canada whom she had recognized? Ah, that was a possibility. A prison guard or physician involved in human rights violations who should have been denied Canadian citizenship and who would lose everything if Eleanor spoke.

Peter put the brakes on this train of imaginative thought. It seemed fanciful. What if Eleanor had just been unfortunate enough to be home during a robbery? But would she have been likely to leave her door unlocked while preparing for suicide? There was no trace of a break-in, according to the police.

He sighed and walked back to the car. He felt better. The lake, the woods: always soothed. On the way home he stopped at his favourite roadside stand and picked up a fresh, warm apple pie.

8

It was the day of Annie's follow-up with Dr. Stone. Based on their previous experience, they decided Jan would take Annie, while Peter would drop Jenny and Liza off at Jan's mother's house for the day. Peter would continue on to Toronto where he had several meetings scheduled.

"Hi, Ruth," he greeted Jan's mum.

"Hi, Peter." Ruth Hutchinson had heard their car pull up and had come out to help unload the girls and their stuff. "Want a coffee?"

Peter grinned at the short, stout figure with its cropped, grey hair. Only the red frames of her glasses hinted that here was no senior going quietly into retirement. "Why, are you afraid of being alone with these two?"

"Ha. It'll take more than Jenny and Liza to scare me." A schoolteacher for most of her working life, Ruth was enjoying her freedom. She had enough time to really focus on making pottery, something she'd come to in the last few years and which she pursued passionately. And time for her only child's children. "How's little Liza?" she asked, lifting the girl from her seat and kissing her.

Jenny, who'd run from the car to the cottage's wide porch where Ruth's orange-striped cat, Marigold, paraded to and fro, scowled and ran back to her grandmother, grabbed her and looked up dramatically. "I need a kiss too," she wailed.

Peter put the diaper bag and assorted toys on the porch, leaned over to pat the cat and refused the offer of coffee. "Too many people to see," he said. "I'm sleeping in Toronto tonight so Jan will pick up these monsters later." He mock-scowled at his daughters, then said his goodbyes.

He'd done the drive to Toronto so many times that he could relax while making all the lane changes and merges that would bring him to the downtown police station where he was to meet the detectives. He breathed deeply and found his mind a blank. So many thoughts and impressions had been working in him for so many weeks that it was restful to just drive and be. He found a parking space and, after some thought, bought the maximum time he could from the meter. He checked his watch and approached the station, a plain grey and glass building set in its own concrete paved plaza. He'd passed it hundreds of times; never thought he'd be entering it on business.

At the window of the small reception area, he stated his business and sat down to wait. After about ten minutes, Smythe appeared behind the window, verified it was he, then came around and opened the door to let him in.

"Thanks for coming. We have some pictures we'd like you to look at. Just check for anyone you might recognize." He seated Peter in a small room with a computer, called up the files he wanted Peter to look at and left.

Peter hadn't really thought of what he might see but wasn't expecting to see pictures of men of all races. He felt quite lost, wondering in what context he should put the faces. Was he meant to be looking for the man who gave him the USB key in Shanghai? For other people he'd seen in China? Or someone he might have seen in Toronto?

Every few minutes he shifted his eyes from the screen to the wall, then resumed his task. He reduced the brightness of the screen. There was one face, but where...? He noted the identification number below the picture on the pad provided on the table, then continued with different faces. He got up and stretched, then returned to the picture: a thin face with thin lips and a receding hairline.

Smythe entered the room with a couple of coffees. "Anything?"

"Well, maybe, but who is he?" Peter pointed to the screen.

"Him? Let's see." Smythe tapped and clicked. "Well, that's interesting. He's a policeman. From — " Here he named the city of Annie's orphanage. Peter's jaw dropped. "But I don't recall a uniform."

"Think outside of that location. Try Fuzhou, Shanghai, the various sights you toured, the airports, the drives to the airports."

Peter's eyes blinked as he recalled the mental picture. "The airport. Leaving Shanghai. The last day in China. This guy. Speaking to Wu, our guide. Watching us. He followed us right to the moment we boarded the plane."

"Okay, that's good."

"But why do you have his picture and file in Toronto?" As Smythe raised his eyebrows and didn't respond, Peter flushed. "Oh, that's one of those questions I shouldn't ask, isn't it?"

Smythe nodded. "Did you finish what I gave you to look at?"

Peter cleared his throat. "Yeah. Yeah, I did. Anything else?"

"Smith and I have looked at your snaps from China. We wonder if you could provide us with a written report, partly based on those pictures, of everything you can remember about the trip." Smythe handed Peter a card. "And send it to this email address."

"I can do that." He hesitated. "I wanted to ask about the phone calls Eleanor received and made on the day she died. You knew about the neighbour hearing her phone ring? Are you able to trace calls? Or is that just a television cop show myth?"

"No, we can trace calls. That one was rather unhelpfully traced to a pay phone at the corner of Bathurst and Bloor."

"Oh. Right near Eleanor's apartment. I didn't even realize there were still pay phones in Toronto."

Smythe grinned. "Not many left, that's for sure."

Peter continued, "Did she make any phone calls that day?"

"Yes, to her lawyer at his home. Cooper said she told him about a new will but not that she had already written it herself. In the event, no such will was found so the old one had to stand."

"So the crucial question is who else did Eleanor tell about a new will, and had she made it and signed it before she was killed?"

"That's about it."

"There's another thing. Who called the ambulance for Eleanor? Who knew she needed help?"

"Dorothy Brandon-Hyde told us when her mother didn't show up at her house, as previously arranged, she phoned her apartment, got no answer and then called emergency. She arrived at the apartment after the paramedics. You seem awfully interested in all this, Mr. Forrest."

"Wouldn't you be, if it was happening within a group of people you knew?"

"I suppose so."

Peter changed the subject. "And how is Smith doing not smoking?"

Smythe seemed surprised Peter had remembered and smiled. "He's got a hold of those electronic cigarettes and claims they're working for him. He still has to go outside for smoke breaks but maybe that's half the attraction. I'll let you out now."

Peter made it back to his car just as the time expired on the meter, added a bit more change and sat at the wheel, exhausted. Now for a nice uncomplicated chat with a friendly lawyer, he thought hopefully, and drove to meet James Cooper.

The lawyer's office shared a building on King Street West with a dentist, an Asian import store and a yoga gym. Peter saw Cooper's name displayed at the end of a list of others, presumably partners, and remembered the lawyer was semi-retired. He walked up to the second floor where a receptionist greeted him. He settled himself to wait, vaguely aware of the girl's pleasant voice answering the phone.

It was an old red brick building on the outside but the interior had apparently been recently gutted and refitted from the bottom up with a shining bamboo floor, a Persian rug, and freshly plastered and painted walls on which were displayed modern abstract paintings. One wall of frosted glass allowed the natural lighting of a sunny summer's day to fill the space, while delicate accent lamps descended on chains from the dimness of the building's original bare timber ceiling.

Peter was surprised. He'd expected Cooper to inhabit a dark den with heavy leather furniture and masses of books. Too many Agatha Christie television adaptations, he thought. Curse you, PBS. So he was prepared, a moment later, for the pleasant, modern room into which the receptionist ushered him.

James Cooper rose and they briefly shook hands. Peter took in the desk, which was actually a polished, modern table, the bookshelves that contained objets d'art as well as books and the pale green curtains that set off the red wallpaper.

"Very nice," he complimented politely.

James laughed. "Not mine. It's a room we keep available for meetings. But thank you. I thought we could have an informal discussion of how you think you are getting on with Eleanor's literary estate and where you think it's heading in the future."

Peter outlined the areas of interest. The poems were shaping up into what promised to be an interesting collection centred on dissidence and its consequences. He mentioned that there were enough poems left to possibly produce a second volume in the future. Then he hesitated.

"I don't know exactly how the other area of Eleanor's work is going to pan out but I have accepted her request to continue her work in human rights, especially as they relate to intellectuals in China."

"Oh, yes."

"I suppose I will be writing about that work in my introduction to the book of poems. Some, I mean most, of the poems are related to that theme. So what seemed like two tasks is becoming one. Does that seem clear to you?"

The lawyer paused. "Yes. I think the family — Dot, really — is just hoping that you'll be able to present Eleanor's last works as part of a continuum, not a radical departure. And that her poetry, not her politics, will dominate."

"Absolutely," said Peter, thinking that "dominate" was an odd word to choose.

The lawyer nodded. He referred to some papers on the desk. "I see you are only charging the estate for your expenses." He looked up at Peter with keen eyes. "Not charging for editing?"

Peter flushed. "Oh, well, I have enough money, and as the work seems to involve a charitable component…"

"Very commendable," the lawyer drily commented.

Peter continued. "I've been questioned by the police with regards to Eleanor's death. Do you have any thoughts on what they're suggesting?"

Peter watched as Cooper's friendly face became blank. "I couldn't comment on anything that relates to Eleanor's death, although I am aware there are some who believe it to have been suspicious. After all," he shrugged and shook his head, "who would want to kill Eleanor?"

"I know. But once you admit the possibility, there are many scenarios that spring to mind."

"Only to those with active imaginations, I'm afraid." The lawyer rose and they shook hands again. "Do keep in touch and send me your expenses, say, every quarter, if you don't mind. Always a pleasure."

"I feel a bit chilled," Peter remarked to the receptionist.

She agreed. "The air conditioning can be a bit much."

On his way back uptown, Peter kept straight past the turnoff for Dot Brandon-Hyde's Rosedale home. It was lunchtime and he wanted something good. He continued over the bridge to the Danforth, parked on a side street and walked to one of his favourite restaurants. He sat in the sidewalk enclosure and waited to be served.

This was his old stomping ground. He'd been raised in a post–Second World War East York bungalow just a few minutes' drive from where he was sitting and a short walk from the Bloor/Danforth subway line. From there, as a youth, and later as a student, all of Toronto was available to him.

He remembered early afternoons at the Carleton Cinema, where he discovered avant-garde movies. He'd walk south on Yonge Street to the book and record stores or north to one of the many taverns and pubs where he could eat and drink for next to nothing. There were late nights with friends when they'd wind up at the only place still open — Fran's — and eat plates of spaghetti and lemon meringue pie.

And after they were married, he and Rachel had rented two storeys of a row house in Riverdale, a rundown neighbourhood south of the Danforth and east of the Don River, so he'd still had access to all his favourite movie houses and restaurants.

He and Jan had simply stayed each in their individual apartments until they'd bought their current house in Dunbarton, married at Toronto Town Hall and moved.

He thought of driving past his parents' old house after lunch but decided he didn't need that bit of sweet pain. It was probably changed anyway. He thought of his parents with affection, wished they could have lived to see him happy with Jan and the girls. He also wished he was more in touch with his sister, Susan, who lived in Vancouver. She was happy with her partner and didn't seem to crave a closer relationship with Peter. Good for her.

He knew it was unfashionable to love Toronto but he did, always had. Maybe when he and Jan were older, and the kids were grown… The waiter arrived with his order: a glass of white wine and a big plate of *mezethes*, appetizers. Eaten with pita bread, they provided the equivalent of a main course and allowed him to sample the menu. He savoured the flavours: dill, lemon, garlic, fish, lamb, cheese. Then dessert: buttery pastry, honey and nuts, coffee.

He knew Cooper would report the details of their meeting to Dot but wanted to discuss things with her in person, so he'd asked for this afternoon's appointment, which had turned into her offering supper and a bed. In the back of his mind was a wish to know Eleanor's daughter better. They'd never been close, as she'd been already married when he first got to know Eleanor personally, as opposed to as a teacher.

Eleanor had moved out of the family home when she got divorced, while Dot had inherited the house when her father, William Brandon, had died.

The Brandon house had been in the family since the nineteenth century. Eleanor had married into and divorced out of a privileged position in Toronto society. Peter wondered how much of that façade Dot bought into.

He also wanted to gently quiz her on her interpretation of the suspicious death inquiry.

He pulled into the double-wide and long driveway (itself a prized element in a Toronto property) and reached for the bouquet he'd picked up at a Korean fruit market near the Greek restaurant. "We're moving up in the world," he quipped to the flowers. Purple, pink and white daisies nodded their agreement.

The house was white with small columns supporting the black porch roof. As he pressed the doorbell he noted the heavy oak door flanked with windows and the gold-edged black numbers of the address etched onto the glass above.

He was relieved to see that the scattered, slightly breathless Dot of Eleanor's funeral had been replaced by someone calm, if still sad-looking. He noticed she was wearing the same bright blue sweater she'd had on after the funeral.

"Come in, come in, Peter, welcome," she said, kissing him on both cheeks and exclaiming with pleasure over the flowers. "So kind of you. Let's pop these into some water. Tea?"

Peter refused her offer as he trailed her into the kitchen. Pine with cast iron black fittings.

"Well, I'm having some, so I'll make a pot. Sit, sit."

He sat at a round glass table on an uncomfortable wrought iron chair with a skimpy green leather seat. "How are you coping, Dot? Are you off for the summer?"

"I'm managing," she smiled. "And I'm off from teaching but not off off. I'm preparing a new course. 'Second Generation Integration: Similarities to and Differences from Immigrating Generation.'" She brought the white teapot to the table and poured her tea into a delicate pale green bone china cup decorated with lilies of the valley.

"Sounds fascinating," he murmured politely. "What are the findings?"

"What you'd expect. Stress, differences in expectations of rewards and in behaviours, the assimilation of the first wave grinding against the necessary, but not always successful, rapid learning curve experienced by the second wave. It's all very applicable to twenty-first-century Toronto and Vancouver and, to a lesser extent, other urban centres across Canada." She laughed. "But your eyes are beginning to glaze, the way mine do when Bill talks about economics. How's your work coming?" Her voice broke a little. "Mum's poems." She pulled the sweater a little closer.

He spoke a little about the proposed book, its structure and content, and how the poems reflected her mother's beliefs and ideals. He also spoke of how the experience was loosening up his creativity, how he was beginning to write poems again, after a long hiatus and, with a lump in his throat, how grateful he felt to Eleanor for this final gift.

Dot leaned forward and touched his hand. "You're really sweet, Peter. I see why Mum loved you."

"We weren't in love, Dot. But we did care for each other."

"Mum told me the reason she broke it off with you was that she was in love with you and she could see you didn't feel the same."

Peter's jaw sagged. "You astonish me. I must have been too young to see or I thought she was so far above me that I never thought something more was possible."

"It wasn't, but her feelings for you were there. You didn't know that you were her last lover?" She rose to take the teapot from the table back to the counter, and as she passed the flowers she'd placed on the granite kitchen island her elbow brushed against them. The lovely crystal vase tipped and shattered on the slate grey tiles. Dot leaned on the island, plucking at a button on the sweater. Peter picked his way through the shards of glass on the floor and brought her back to sit at the table.

"Are you ill, Dot?"

"A little dizzy, a bit breathless."

"Where are the broom and dustpan?" Peter swept up the glass and then dried the floor with paper towels. The flowers were intact and Dot pointed him to a cupboard where he found another vase. He chose one in blue and white porcelain, positioning it in the centre of the island.

"Sometimes I'm nauseous too. My doctor says it's probably menopause. You know, hormones. Like when you're pregnant." She cheered up as she added sarcastically, "It's so much fun being a woman. What were we talking about?"

"It doesn't matter. Why don't you have a rest, Dot? I wouldn't mind some quiet time before supper."

Dot rose. "I'll show you to your room and then I think I will have a lie-down."

As he followed her up the stairs, Peter noticed her left hand gripping the banister and wondered if she was more ill than she said. She left him at the door of his room.

He put his gym bag on a chair and went to look out one of the two dormer windows. Dot's was a pleasant street with mature trees that muffled the afternoon hum of traffic. He peeked into the adjoining bathroom. It was beautifully appointed with an antique tub, heated towel rail and a selection of high-end toiletries as well as having its own view — of the sky through a smaller window, the lower half of which was pebbled for modesty's sake, its upper half tilted open for air.

No lack of money here, thought Peter ruefully, remembering his and Jan's downstairs bathroom with its rotten floor, the run-on toilet, the ventilation problems. He hoped the handyman would show up in August to make their modest improvements. He lay on the bed with some poems to revise and spent a contented couple of hours before dozing off briefly.

Around 5:30 he awoke, showered, shaved, and went downstairs. He could hear Dot working in the kitchen but instead of joining her went into the living room, a large, gracious room with a high ceiling and the ornamental plaster and woodwork Peter associated with Victorian design, painted a pale Wedgwood blue with white trim. The furniture was elegant: not Victorian, but from an earlier period, with clean lines and silver patterned upholstery. Sheer drapes maintained privacy facing the street, while French doors opened onto the back garden.

Peter examined the array of family photos arranged on the shining wood of a side table. Dot had chosen not to display Eleanor and William Brandon's wedding picture, if such a thing existed. Peter grinned at the thought of Eleanor posing in a long white dress, train draped artistically in front, with hubby at her side. There was such a picture on display but it was of Dot and Bill.

Confusing that Dot's father and husband were both Williams. But perhaps William Brandon was always called William while Bill Hyde preferred Bill.

Dot did have two separate shots of her parents and had arranged them on her side of her wedding photo while Bill's parents' picture (of the two seated together) was on Bill's side.

Peter picked up and held Eleanor's picture. She was young, possibly still an undergraduate, and her face had that dreamy, hooded quality some young women possess for a time. Before life wakes them up, he thought. What if he'd been her contemporary? Anything might have been possible.

"A lovely woman, my mother-in-law," remarked Bill, striding into the room. "Drink?" He poured himself a Scotch. "God, I'm glad that day is done." He loosened and removed his tie. He looked tired, not so much the svelte, handsome banker Peter remembered from the funeral.

"Tough one? I'll have what you're having." Peter nodded in the direction of Bill's glass.

"They're all tough since the recession. Anyway, mustn't complain. Canadian banks are sitting pretty compared to the Americans'." He brought Peter his drink. "Your health." They clinked glasses and sat down.

"Dot doesn't need a hand?"

"God, no. She's got her glass of wine and she's happily concocting something delicious for us. She's a pretty good cook."

"How's she managing, with the grief, I mean, and the winding down of the estate?"

"Well, the estate is being liquidated by Cooper, of course, and very competent he is too. Although I could have done the job for Eleanor. She didn't want that, Eleanor." He rose and refilled his glass, checking that Peter's didn't need a top-up. "The grief—Dot's seemed a bit better lately but now she gets these dizzy spells. I don't think her doctor really knows what's wrong with her." He leaned forward and lowered his voice, looking worried. "She's been acting a bit strange, forgetting things, dropping things. It's almost like she's not quite there sometimes. Do people get senility in their forties? Maybe she's bipolar."

Shocked, Peter replied, "No, I don't think so. She's emotionally tired and working on something for the fall semester. Perhaps she needs a holiday."

"We decided to skip a holiday this summer. But how about you? You've just returned from China, haven't you? What did you think of the place?"

"Polluted, crowded, noisy, busy. Capable of great beauty and great ugliness."

"They're the coming nation. The nation of the twenty-first century, in my belief. America is finished. We'd do better to ally ourselves with China."

"Isn't that the trend already?"

"We could do more in that direction. Invest. Open up new markets for our oil and pulp. Their lack of regulation offers unique opportunities for research and development."

"You sound as if you're an expert."

"I've made it my business to become one," Bill said grimly. "If you don't keep up with trends" — he drew his finger across his throat—"you get eaten alive."

Dot appeared in the entrance of the room. "I thought we could just eat in the kitchen tonight as the kids are out and Peter is almost family." She gave him a smile.

"Where are the kids?" asked Bill as they ate their chicken pot pie.

"Jeana's at Gabby's house — we have to pick her up around nine — and Max has hockey. His coach will bring him home as usual."

"Should I sober up?" asked Bill, reaching for the second bottle of Chardonnay and offering it around before filling his own glass.

Peter, who didn't really like Chardonnay and really, really didn't like this one, which proclaimed its cheapness by the dominant scent and subsequent taste of sweat, offered to go. "Is it close by?"

"Very good of you, Peter, to offer, but I'll go," said Dot.

"Yes, very good of you, Good Peter." Bill laughed and dropped his fork.

Dot picked it up and brought him a clean one.

"Thank you, my wife, my good wife." He turned to Peter. "You got a good wife, Peter? What's 'er name?"

"Jan," said Peter, not really wanting to discuss her with Bill in his current state.

"Jan, Jan. Have I ever met her? She pretty, your good wife?"

"I think so," Peter responded, thinking of Jan's sturdy body, her plain face with its sweet expression.

"Bill, do you want dessert?"

"No, gonna watch TV," said Bill, rising and then heading off to his study.

Dot cleared their plates, then brought fruit salad and cheese. They ate in silence.

"Very nice dinner," Peter managed to say.

Dot put down her spoon. "I suppose you think I'm weak," she said, "to stay. To put up with it."

"Look, Dot…" he began.

"He's never violent. He's a happy drunk. It's when he doesn't drink that he gets mean. Just verbally: sarcastic, embarrasses the kids. That's why they avoid him, us. They don't know which way he's going to go."

Peter murmured, "I'm so sorry, Dot."

"I told Mum. Well, she could see for herself when she visited. She didn't like it so she avoided visiting, at least when Bill would be around. Or sometimes I'd visit her. She was supposed to visit the day she died. I miss her." She leaned her head on the palms of her hands as a few tears dropped. She rubbed them into the sweater.

Peter briefly touched her arm. "So you called your mother the day she died?"

"Yes. She was two hours late. She must have switched her answering machine off. The phone rang and rang and then I phoned emergency. When I got there the paramedics were still working on her. It was dreadful." She paused. "Do you think someone murdered Mum?" she asked wildly.

"The police tell me it's likely, but I have no idea who they suspect."

"They suspect me," she said, calming down. "They've been here several times for discussions — about money, mostly."

"Is money a problem?"

"Yes, no. I don't really know. Bill handles the investing for us. He says there's enough between his job and my trust fund. But my trust fund pays for everything: the house — there's no mortgage, of course — but upkeep, the kids' activities, groceries. I don't know what Bill does with his money. He says he's 'planning our retirement.'"

"It's quarter to nine. Should you get Jeana?"

"Oh, listen to me, bothering you with all my worries. It's just…I used to tell Mum." She plucked at the blue sweater with her fingers. "This was hers. It was hanging on the chair at her desk."

"Well, listen, call me if you need to talk. I mean it." He got up and thanked her for dinner. "Good night."

Whew, he thought, climbing the stairs to his room, I can't wait to get home.

He rose early and went for a walk around the neighbourhood. He let his mind relax and absorb the stately homes in their quiet surroundings, the extra strip of lawn between sidewalk and pavement that transformed street into boulevard. Privilege, he supposed. A matter of birth in some cases, of hard work and luck in others.

He smiled when he contrasted the size of the Rosedale houses with that of his childhood home. The tiny front room with the dining room behind it and a galley kitchen squeezed to one side of the bungalow's central hallway. The two little bedrooms in the back. A nice-sized yard, though, for his mother's roses and dahlias.

He reached for the little green notebook and pencil, stopped on the sidewalk and wrote, walked a few more paces and wrote again, and so on, until the poem emerged.

On his return, Dot was having breakfast with the kids. Max was a big, heavy boy who mumbled his hello. Jeana, who seemed to have inherited some of her father's confidence, looked at Peter with bright, curious eyes. Peter refused Dot's offer to join them and, pleading a meeting at work, made his way to the university.

There was no meeting. He just wanted to check his office. He hadn't been in since before the China trip. As he drove through the campus, he thought for the hundredth time how unprepossessing it looked: modern, utilitarian buildings with a landscape that, however generous it might be, was curiously barren. He parked and entered his building, descended into the sub-basement, unlocked the door, then closed it behind him and stepped into the depressing little space.

At least there didn't seem to be any obvious trashing of his books and papers. Things were a bit mixed up: the books replaced haphazardly on the shelves, the papers and files stacked on his desk. He wondered how it had looked when security and then the police had arrived. Not for the first time, he wished for an office above ground or, at least, if he had to be in the basement, one with a window at eye level.

He spent the morning reordering the room, then drove home. He realized he'd completely forgotten Annie's follow-up appointment the previous day. Rats. Be a father first, he admonished himself.

9

"So how was the lovely Dorothy?" Jan looked up from mopping the kitchen tiles. "Still thin and rich?" She grinned impishly at Peter, who was emptying the dishwasher.

"Sad and maybe not so rich."

"Really." She paused and leaned on her mop.

"She misses her mother and she doesn't know where her husband's money is going. Bill has a drinking problem."

"Uh-oh." Jan dunked the mop into the soapy bucket and pushed down once or twice. Her father had been a drunk and it had ended her parents' marriage.

"So explain what Dr. Stone had to say again? I'm confused. Two scars, one kidney?"

Jan paused again and stood upright. "The scar on the left side is old and that's where the kidney is. The scar on the right is fresher, maybe three to four months old. The list is in my office," she said.

"List?"

"The list of things to watch out for with Annie. That Dr. Stone gave me." Jan's "office" was a wooden desk tray for large documents and a small basket jammed with receipts and pens in one corner of the kitchen counter.

Peter skimmed, then read it aloud. "Avoid contact sports, check-ups four times a year, watch for more or less amounts of urine, watch for flu-like symptoms. Huh. So no soccer."

Jan went outside with the bucket. Peter heard a swoosh as the water drenched an old-fashioned shrub rose at the side of the house: Jan's treatment for aphids. He raised his voice. "She can play tennis. They all can."

When Jan didn't reappear he followed her out to where she was watching Jenny playing in the dirt pile out back. Liza and Annie were napping.

"Our problem child," Jan softly said.

"It's just her age. They all get tantrums at three or four." He'd witnessed some doozies emanating from Jenny's classmates when dropping her off at preschool. "It'll pass."

"You think?"

"Be glad the others seem of calmer dispositions."

"Be glad they still nap, you mean. 'Of calmer dispositions'? You sound like Jane Austen."

"Wow, you really know how to build up a guy's masculinity."

"Doesn't need any building up," she teased. "You remember I'm going out this aft and again tonight?"

"Oh, yeah, it's your mother's thing."

The thing was a regional arts and crafts show at Dunbarton's tiny community centre. Ruth lived in nearby Catchton, which, like many of the surrounding villages, was barely large enough to support a combination grocery/hardware/post office: the GHPO, as its natives called it. Peter thought the letters stood for 'God Has Pissed Off' but kept that private. It was his mother-in-law's hamlet, after all.

Jan had volunteered to help her mother pack her pottery and then unpack it in the centre's hall. Then the two women would have supper with Peter and the girls before returning for the opening that evening.

"Do you want to come tonight? Free wine and nibbles. I can try to get a sitter."

"I'll look in tomorrow during the day. Or Sunday. I have to write that report for the cops."

"All right. I should go. I'll just say goodbye to Jenny." She handed Peter the empty bucket.

Peter watched his wife walk over and crouch next to their daughter. Jenny didn't look up and seemed to be engrossed in her game, submitting, not responding to Jan's kiss.

"Watch out," muttered Jan as she passed Peter, giving him a quick kiss.

He ambled back into the kitchen, thought about supper, checked he had a large frozen lasagne and went out to the garden to see if the peas were in yet. Beautiful. He picked both kinds, popping the sweet edible-podded ones into his mouth as he moved up and down the rows, dropping the ones that had to be shelled into a large bowl.

The vegetable garden was mostly his responsibility. He'd been entranced by the writings of various northern gardeners who saw the shorter growing season as a challenge and a blessing. The shorter season meant fewer pests than were attracted to southern gardens. By diversifying what he planted and when, he gave the family free produce for a good six months of the year. "Everything from asparagus in May to pumpkins in October," he'd brag to anyone who'd listen. He knew he was a garden bore but didn't care.

So here he was at the end of June, picking peas, surveying his lettuces like some younger version of the Mr. McGregor who appeared in the Peter Rabbit books he and Jan read to the girls. Deer were a rare nuisance but the rabbits were a menace, especially in spring. Thus the low chicken-wire fence he'd cobbled together using leftover lumber and sticks. It was either that or a cat, but he'd seen the damage Ruth's cat could inflict on mice, birds, and, once, a baby rabbit. He didn't want that on his conscience.

He rinsed and refrigerated the produce, then took a juice box out to Jenny. She sipped in silence while they both regarded her game.

She'd dug a long central trench and, on either side, a series of holes. Each hole contained a few sticks except for one that contained only one stick.

"Are you planting?" asked Peter, fresh from his gardening.

"No." Jenny sucked her juice box dry and flung it away.

"Hey, we don't do that. Pick it up."

Jenny stomped over to the box and brought it to Peter.

"Thank you," he said softly. "Want to tell me about your game?"

"No," she replied shortly.

"I'll go work in my study then."

Jenny resumed her excavations.

Peter sat on the couch and watched her for a bit before taking up his Chinese journal. He'd use it as a basis for his report to Smith and Smythe.

He took the first entry, the meeting with and description of Lin Huiyin, the first guide, in Fuzhou, jotted it down, then closed his eyes and let the impressions of the moment surface.

But clear impressions wouldn't surface. Lin, Chen, Wu, the adoption agency director — his contact with them had been so brief, how could his brain sort it out?

Images came: of the waterfalls cascading down the hill behind the orphanage, the bus idling behind the military base next to the orphanage, the thin-faced stranger talking to Wu at the airport. He wondered why he hadn't given much thought to the blond man who'd given him the USB key in the garden grotto in Shanghai.

The bus idling behind the orphanage. He opened the computer and revisited some human rights abuse sites. On one, buses were used to house prisoners being executed by lethal injection: mobile organ harvesting. He recalled his photo of the bus. He clicked on the file and found it. He'd been shooting the manicured front courtyard of the orphanage from the roof and there was the bus, behind the wall separating the courtyard from the military building and its parking lot. Was there a child in the bus while he took the picture? A prisoner? A death?

He wrote.

He wrote about Lin, a serious and reserved woman who'd seemed to relax as they left the city and entered the countryside. She'd enjoyed the boat ride upriver to the small town where they'd lunched. Then, back in Fuzhou, she'd shut down again. Maybe she was originally a countrywoman or maybe she'd been frightened.

So, next came the adoption itself. Five people and Peter.

He discounted the two civil servants. They were paper-shufflers, rubber-stampers. All he'd taken from them was the dignity of the senior man sitting behind the desk and the obsequious attention paid him by his junior.

The orphanage director and Annie's nanny: one in her power suit, the other in baggy grey sweat pants and smock. The director not once making direct eye contact with Peter even when he gave her the gift of whisky; the nanny with some nervousness in her manner, a wariness in her eyes.

And Annie. Not resembling the little girl in the adoption file photograph. Darker skin, a round instead of long face. He wondered if Lin Huiyin had been in on the deception too. He hoped not.

The first time he changed Annie's diaper, a few hours after they returned to the hotel room. Touching the scar, thinking he was imagining things, rereading the child's file and finding no mention of distinguishing birthmarks or scars. This uneasiness accompanied by a growing feeling of protectiveness toward his new daughter.

He replayed the events of the day's visit to Annie's orphanage in his mind. A silent drive, arrival, check-in with the office next door, the beauty of the spot, taking photos from the ground, then from the roof, laundry flapping, the children. God, the children: playing, drinking; the small beds in the large rooms. Walking downstairs. The alarm, the surgical team, his turning away, controlling his shock. His rationalization that the surgeons were there to help the children. Soldiers rushing to put out a fire. The drive to the airport. His relief at leaving his driver, Chen. His relief at leaving that city.

He wondered if, because of what he'd seen at the orphanage, he'd been followed from that point on. Had someone been tailing them as they visited the tourist sights of Fuzhou, shadowing them as they twisted through the narrow streets of the old town district? Or had that been Lin's job, to spy and report?

Had someone been watching him and Josh on their brief walk out the first evening in Shanghai? He noted what he could remember of the police activity in the park near their hotel as several men were chased and arrested. And had he been observed the next day as he walked in the smog of Shanghai, mingling with tourists along the riverside boulevard?

He noted that there had been a day's delay at the Canadian consulate with regard to completing Annie's papers that had resulted in his meeting with Macdonald. He wondered what he should say about that. He also wondered whose eyes would ultimately view the present report he was compiling.

At this point in his ruminations he heard a little cry from upstairs and thankfully put his journal and laptop down. Back to life, he thought.

Between looking after the girls and preparing supper, eating supper with Jan and Ruth, listening to their excited gossip about fellow exhibitors, and putting the girls to bed, it was eight o'clock that evening before he re-entered his study and re-engaged with his memories.

Macdonald. What was that all about? Peter had suppressed mention of Annie's scar and of seeing the surgical team at the time because he was anxious there be no delay in leaving China. He thought for a moment, then included the latter incident in his report. He described Macdonald as best he could: tall, greying brown hair, grey eyes.

He supposed the next significant thing was the gay pride fun-run and being contacted by one of the runners. He focused on the blond Asian man and tried to itemize elements of his appearance. He remembered the man had a chipped front tooth, revealed when he smiled at Annie and handed her a candy. He remembered his own fear and he remembered something else. He jotted it down.

He concluded by describing his purchase of similar USBs at the electronics store and his destruction of one of the new ones by fire at City God Temple. He briefly mentioned the watcher at Shanghai Airport and that the man had been identified as a Chinese policeman.

He exhaled forcefully as he pressed send and heard Jan come in. "Cheese breath," he murmured as they kissed.

The next morning Peter watched *The Dying Rooms*.

He'd known of the movie. It had been made years ago, but he had avoided watching it, feeling too squeamish. Then, when he and Jan had committed to adopting their first Chinese child, he'd felt he didn't need to. Jan had seen it and had been distracted for a few days after. "Strong stuff," she'd told him. Now he felt he needed to know.

The state-run orphanages. The toddlers tied to their potty chairs, the obsessive rocking of some, passivity of others. The handicapped and disfigured kids. The older children interacting roughly with the younger, sometimes hitting them repeatedly. The dying child. The child put in a room to die. Her emaciated body, crusty eyes. Her weak cry. Her name: Mei Ming, meaning, no name. No name, no name.

The really sad thing was the section of the film that contrasted conditions in state-run orphanages with private ones funded through charities. The kids in the latter were freer to move around, seemed happier. So it was possible. Money made the difference.

He quietly left the house, drove over to the community centre and looked at the paintings, pottery, wooden pens, duck decoys and birdhouses displayed on long tables crammed together in the small space. He greeted his mother-in-law, who looked excited and happy, and bought a medium-sized jug from her and a hand-turned wooden pen from another vendor. Both would make nice gifts.

The turnout was pretty good. Little kids, on the loose, ran from table to table, clutching loonies and toonies, looking for some little thing to buy. Tourists and locals mingled, snacked at the volunteer-run counter: all proceeds going to worthy local charities. He ate a hotdog and drank a coffee, waved goodbye to Ruth, went and sat in his car and listened to a report on murdered and missing indigenous women and girls in British Columbia.

So much to do. Not just Falun Gong but the most helpless everywhere needed advocacy. There'd been nothing about children in Eleanor's files. This would be his own thing, he decided.

The next six weeks were a blur of solitary research and reading mingled with days in the garden and with Jan and the kids.

Jenny behaved herself, more or less, while Liza made a breakthrough in speaking. These two now conversed almost unceasingly. "I feel my ears bleeding," Peter confided to Jan after listening to them chattering all of one day spent at the beach.

Annie continued her quiet existence though she tired easily. She accepted their affection but didn't seem to reciprocate it.

The handyman finally came and tore out the main floor bathroom. The renovation dragged on as he flitted from one job location to another. They were frustrated by having to share one bathroom but told themselves it was temporary. More than once, Peter found himself peeing in the bushes at the side of the house. He'd talked about peeing around the edge of the vegetable garden to deter the critters but the idea had been nixed by Jan. He was just zipping up one fine August morning, thinking of picking some tomatoes, eggplant and zucchini for ratatouille, when he heard the sound of a car arriving. He came around the corner of the house to see Smith and Smythe getting out.

"Hello. What's up?"

Smith had an electronic cigarette jammed into his mouth and a frown pasted onto his forehead. "Need to ask you some questions."

Peter nodded to Smythe and led the way to his study. They passed the two eldest girls watching television in the living room. Jan was upstairs with Annie. Peter went up to tell her what was happening, then went back down to the kitchen and prepared a coffee tray. Once back in the study he closed the door. "Has something happened?"

Smythe went first. "First of all, we received your China report, read it and forwarded it to the appropriate government agency along with your photographs."

"Am I allowed to know which agency?" Peter asked.

"CSIS, and from there it will probably be sent to and read by various government departments. Secondly, we'd like to know more about your relationship with the people involved in the Eleanor Brandon case."

"It's a case, then?"

Smith accepted his coffee and stirred in the cream. "Oh, yes, it's a case, all right." He sounded grim.

Smythe resumed. "We want to know about your dealings with James Cooper and Bill Hyde."

"My dealings?"

"Meetings, what was said."

Peter recounted his meetings with James Cooper at Eleanor's funeral, at her apartment and at Cooper's office. "That's it," he concluded, "except for a few phone calls about the business of the estate."

"Oh? The estate?"

Peter could hear the suspicion in Smith's voice. "The literary estate. I'm Eleanor's literary executor. I don't get paid. Just the cost of gas or a hotel room if I have to stay in town, though it's just been gas so far."

"Yes. Hotel rooms. We understand the last time you had a meeting with Mr. Cooper you stayed at the Brandon-Hyde residence."

Peter was surprised. "Is this about fraud or something? I assure you I won't be charging the estate for a fictitious hotel room."

Smith sucked at his cigarette, blew the vapour into the room. Peter wondered if he should object for the girls' sake. These cigarettes hadn't really been proved harmless yet. He looked at Smith's fractious expression and decided to let it ride. "Not fraud but murder, Mr. Forrest."

Smythe brought their attention back to the subject. "And how have you found Mr. Cooper?"

"All right. Friendly at first. Then a little cooler as things have gone on. Professional, I guess."

"And Mr. Hyde? What's your impression of him?"

"Well, I only met him for the first time at the funeral, like Cooper. He's Dot's husband but I really don't know him. He seems to have a drinking problem. Dot told me...should I be discussing Mrs. Brandon-Hyde's marital difficulties, I wonder?"

"We would very much like to hear about Mrs. Brandon-Hyde's marital difficulties," Smythe replied smoothly. "And about your relations with her."

"My relations?" Peter heard his own voice sounding incredulous. "What is this? I don't have any 'relations' with Dot Brandon-Hyde. I knew her mother, not Dot." Then, as the officers remained silent, he added, "I would like to know her better now because I feel sorry for her. She's grieving her mother's death. Murder. And her husband's a drunk."

Smythe quietly interjected, "Mrs.Brandon-Hyde is a lovely woman."

"What's that supposed to mean? I love my wife and I am not attracted to Dot except as a friend."

Smith spoke in bored tones. "William Hyde was found dead at his home yesterday. It is thought he asphyxiated while choking on his vomit. He was found by his teenaged daughter. In his study. With a taped plastic bag over his head."

Peter blanched. He stood up and went to look out the window where he observed a breeze rustling the leaves of the backyard trees, shifting the patterns of dappled shade they made on the lawn. "Poor Bill. Poor girl," he murmured.

Smith continued. "There was a note claiming he'd killed Eleanor when she spoke of leaving her money to charity instead of to Dot. Turns out Bill Hyde made a lot of iffy investments before 2008, not just with his own money but with that of his clients. His company found out and agreed not to prosecute as long as he made good. He was skint."

Peter turned to face the detectives. "Why are you telling me this?" He was bewildered.

"Because you have associated with the Hydes and their lawyer recently and we suspect you may have an interest in Eleanor Brandon's money or daughter or both," Smith snapped.

"That's disgusting and untrue."

"Only a suspicion, Mr. Forrest," said Smythe. He looked at his partner as if reminding him of that as well. "Only a suspicion. Thank you for your cooperation."

As Peter showed the men out, they passed Jan and the girls sitting silently. Peter saw by Jan's white face that she'd heard part if not all of the conversation.

10

As the end of August approached, Peter rushed to finish Eleanor's book. He wrote the introductory essay and sent the finished manuscript to Eleanor's long-time publisher with relief. He now had to prep his courses and deal with meetings and paperwork related to his university job.

Jenny began kindergarten, Liza began half-days at Jenny's old preschool and Jan spent her mornings at home with Annie before picking up Liza at lunchtime and Jenny after school. It meant a lot of driving for everybody but both Jan and Peter had known driving — chauffeuring kids and commuting — was one of the necessary aspects of living in the country. The days were so busy and the evenings so brief that the familial intimacy achieved by summer's more relaxed pace dissipated somewhat, though they made time to pick apples and visit a combination corn maze and pumpkin patch. Jan focused on the kids, Peter on his various work commitments. He was also writing letters as part of his human rights work — letters asking Canadian politicians to put pressure on the Chinese government to improve conditions of children in orphanages and for members of the Falun Gong and other dissidents, with special reference to forced organ donations.

The hours he spent harvesting vegetables and closing down the garden were among his best. Fresh compost spread over the empty beds held the promise of renewed growth next spring. And he wasn't getting any younger. Winter offered more freedom to rest, at least from the physical chores outside the house.

The Saturday of Thanksgiving weekend, Ruth volunteered to take the kids for the day. Peter and Jan drove to Gananoque, a nearby waterfront village, and had lunch at the pub there. Jan brought up the police investigation of Eleanor's and Bill's deaths. Peter, who had lately had no time to do more than vaguely wonder how it was going, was surprised. He thought Jan had forgotten all about it.

"The case must be wrapped up. They must accept Bill did it," Peter assured her. "Get me that ketchup from the table behind you, would you?"

"Still, it's unusual that two people you know have recently died — one, murdered; the other, the murderer."

Peter shook ketchup on his french fries. "But there's an end to it. How's Annie today, do you think?"

"I don't know. She can't get rid of that cough and she doesn't seem to want to do anything. I'm a bit worried."

"See Dr. Stone?"

"I made an appointment for next week."

"Well, that's all you can do. Now, how about dessert? Mmm. Rhubarb crumble."

Jan smiled. "You twisted my arm. After all, we are celebrating our brand new bathroom."

Peter felt a frisson of pleasure every time he entered the fresh yellow-and-white-painted room. Finally, a grey slate floor instead of cracked and shrinking vinyl, a fan, and new fixtures instead of the old stained ones. He and Jan never argued over who had to clean in there: they were both still loving the change.

They walked the pretty streets of the town, read the historical plaques on houses and in the park, took a look at the lake, and wondered if they could prevail on Ruth to sleep over at their house if they checked into a bed and breakfast. Eventually they decided it was asking too much of her and drove home.

Ruth met them at the door, holding Annie. "Feel her forehead, Jan. I think she's running a little fever. I couldn't find your thermometer."

Jan touched Annie's forehead and her flushed cheeks. "Are the others okay?"

"They seem fine," Peter reported, returning downstairs with the thermometer. "Hmm. A hundred. That's not so bad."

"Yeah, but remember the list, Peter. A hundred for a normal kid could be worse for Annie."

"Do you need me to stay?" asked Ruth. "Because I can."

"No, no, Ruth, you go home. We'll call you if we need you."

Ruth let herself out and Jan and Peter took Annie up to their room. Jan undid her diaper. "Peter, it's dry. Stop Mum."

Peter ran downstairs and caught Ruth in her car still in the driveway. "Ruth, when did you last change her diaper?"

Ruth thought. "Well, I changed Liza after lunch and checked Annie then but it was dry and then checked them both around four but Liza used the potty instead and Annie's was still dry. Is that bad?"

"Could be. Safe drive home."

Peter rummaged around in the kitchen drawer where they kept all the kids' health records and looked at the list entitled "Symptoms of kidney failure."

Urinating more or less often. Check. Feeling very tired. Check. Annie wasn't showing any of the other symptoms: loss of appetite, nausea, vomiting, swelling hands or feet, itchiness or numbness, darkened skin, muscle cramps. Of course, she couldn't tell them if she felt sick or itchy or numb. He reread the list, then took it upstairs.

"Hey, Jan," he began.

"Hmm?" She was bathing Annie's face with a cool wet facecloth and offering her little sips of apple juice.

"It doesn't say anything on here about a fever. Maybe she has an infection or the flu?"

"Maybe. Let's wait until tomorrow and see."

But by midnight, when Annie still hadn't peed and was starting to cry off and on, Jan made up her mind. "I'm taking her to the hospital. Something's wrong."

After they'd left, Peter prowled around the house. He couldn't sleep. The hospital was fifteen minutes away and he figured a fevered baby with one kidney might take priority in emergency ahead of the broken bones and other minor ailments. Sure enough, around one Jan called.

"They catheterized her and nothing came out. They think there's no urine moving through the kidney. Her ankles are starting to swell and the fever's mounting. They're pretty sure the kidney is sick," she gulped, "if not failing, so she's going on dialysis right away. I'll stay here." She added in a smaller voice, "Can you come?"

Peter called Ruth and apologized for waking her. "Your instincts were right," he said. "Can you come stay with Jenny and Liza while I join Jan?"

"Of course, dear. I'll pack a few things and be right over."

It was two by the time Peter reached Jan and Annie. Annie was having dialysis and had been given a sedative. A weary Jan greeted him.

"They still don't understand the fever but are testing for infections. They want to do a kidney biopsy. I said okay." Peter grimaced as she continued. "It's just a needle. She shrieked when the doctor pressed on the kidney. He said that's not usual either."

"Why don't you take a break? Walk around, drink something, or close your eyes for a few minutes. I'll watch her."

They took turns at Annie's bedside. At one point Jan went out to the car and slept for a few hours. Peter just kept sipping the awful coffee from the hospital vending machines, then finally switched to hot chocolate.

The next day was Thanksgiving Sunday. Jan went home for a shower and a nap in the morning. Peter went home in the afternoon and slept until after supper. Ruth had found their turkey in the fridge and roasted it along with some carrots and potatoes. She and Jenny and Liza had made cookies. Jan slept at home that night and took over at the hospital Monday morning when Peter came home to rest. By Wednesday, the tests had been done and the doctor, one of the doctors, had a brief meeting with both of them.

"We definitely have total organ function failure. But the thing is that we believe the kidney that has just failed was a donated kidney and that what we're seeing is rejection by the body of the donated organ. Are you familiar with what happens when the recipient's immune system attacks the new kidney? Good. So, this kidney is done. The first thing to do is to get Annie stabilized, on an organ recipient list and a dialysis schedule."

"But if she was an organ recipient, shouldn't she have been on drugs to prevent organ rejection?" Jan is obviously more alert than I am, thought Peter tiredly.

"Yes, normally, but some new research suggests some patients may be gradually weaned off of these immunosuppressive drugs, which, as you may know, sometimes have serious side effects."

"So why can't you give her some immunosuppressive drugs now?" asked Peter.

"We tried that once we realized we were dealing with rejection, but I'm afraid the kidney is already damaged. It was weak and probably became infected. We may have to remove it." Jan muffled a groan. "That can be done here and dialysis is available here. A transplant would ideally happen at the children's hospital in Toronto sometime in the future. We can help with blood tests and tissue typing would-be donors. You'll want to donate a kidney if possible?"

"Yes, of course," they both replied.

"Good. So we'll probably get that old kidney out as soon as possible and guide you through the next steps. All right?"

"Thank you, Doctor," they murmured.

"One day at a time," Peter reassured Jan, giving her a hug. "She'll be okay."

Surgery was performed on Annie two days after the discussion.

Peter rearranged his workload for the rest of that semester, switching courses with another professor so he was only needed two days a week. He and Jan shared the three times weekly dialysis appointments for Annie, each one lasting about four hours, as well as caring for the other two kids. Ruth was great, helping with babysitting and rides when needed. Some of the parents at Liza's preschool and Jenny's school helped as well, giving lifts home or taking the girls for a few hours at their homes.

Peter knew Halloween was coming when their local grocery store decorated its windows and set out all the candy by its entrance. He bought only a small amount plus three costumes in what he thought were roughly the right sizes. Because of their rural location and the ages of the girls, Peter and Jan were spared the necessity of having to go door-to-door; instead the girls were satisfied with the activities at their schools during the day and wearing their costumes at home. Jennie was a witch, Liza a princess, while a mystified Annie was a bunny.

Peter, Jan and Ruth were first blood- then tissue-typed over a period of a few weeks. By the beginning of November when the results came in, they knew they didn't match. They would have to wait for a donor. The average wait time was one to two years.

When Jenny heard that Annie needed a new kidney and understood that the doctors would take one from one person and put it into Annie, she got very quiet. Then she burst out with "I don't want to give stupid Annie a stupid kidney!" and rushed off to her room.

Peter followed her there to find her crying into her pillow.

"Jenny, Jenny," he gently admonished. "Little kids don't have to give their organs. It might make them sick. Only grown-ups like me and Mummy or Gramma Ruth."

"You like her better than me. Stupid Annie. I hope she dies." She resumed her wailing.

"No, you don't, Jenny. Who would you play with? Who would you teach to say her ABCs? We love all you girls the same and Annie needs her big sister when she feels sick. And Mummy and Daddy need you just because you're our first child and very special to us. Soon you'll have your birthday and we'll have a party with all your friends." He soothed her and carried her back downstairs to the living room where the other two were waiting, pushed a DVD into the machine and went to pop some corn. Jan was sitting at the kitchen table.

"I have never been so utterly weary before in my life," she said, laying her head down along her outstretched arm on the table.

"Here, have some popcorn."

"I'd rather have wine."

"You may have wine." He took two glasses and an opened bottle of wine and passed them to her. "Come on. Let's join the girls. A very funny movie is being shown tonight, judging by the laughs coming from the other room."

Some adoptive parents had parties on the days that commemorated their first meetings with their children but Peter and Jan had never been comfortable making a big deal of the fact that the kids were adopted and stuck to celebrating birthdays. Jenny's fifth was November 13th and they had a party the following Saturday with just a half dozen kids from her class. Peter bought balloons and favours and picked up a cake while Jan cleaned the house and prepared the children. The party culminated in Jenny having a meltdown of tremendous proportions as she realized that that day wasn't her real birthday.

"But, sweetie, on your real birthday we brought cupcakes to school, remember?" Jan was trying to calm Jenny and separate her from the other children who were beginning to look nervous. Peter had a feeling Jenny wasn't exactly well liked at school.

Jan continued, "So you had two birthdays, didn't you?" Eventually, and due to the distraction of the cake arriving, ablaze with five candles (and one extra for good luck), Jenny settled down, but she wouldn't let the other children touch her new toys. By the time it was all over, the family was exhausted and glad that the Christmas holidays were fast approaching.

About a week before Christmas Annie caught a cold, which turned into pneumonia. She was so ill she was brought to the Toronto children's hospital. Jan and Peter took a room in a nearby hotel so they would have a place to shower and rest. The next few days passed in a blur of napping and hospital visiting until one morning, when Peter was sleeping alone at the hotel, the phone rang and, as expected, he heard Ruth's voice. Only she, Peter and Jan had the number. They'd tried to keep a low profile; everyone was busy with Christmas. "What's up, Ruth?" he croaked.

"Well, you got a phone message I thought you'd like to know about. I'm sorry I woke you."

"That's all right," he mumbled. "Should be getting up anyway. Who called?"

"Well, it's the daughter of that friend of yours who was murdered—Dorothy Brandon-Hyde, she said. I wouldn't have bothered you except she sounded needy, if you know what I mean."

She gave him the number and he called. Dot was sorry to hear about his daughter but could he come to her house? She had something important to discuss.

He went to the hospital and found Jan sitting with Annie. "How is she this morning?" he asked.

"About the same. It's slow because she's already weak from the dialysis."

"When would you like your break, love? Because I could go now to see Dot Brandon-Hyde. She called about something to do with Eleanor."

"Geez, can't it wait? We've got a sick kid here."

"I just thought that seeing as we're already in the city I could get it over with so when we're home again we can just cocoon over the holidays." He clasped his wife's hand. "I know this has been a struggle."

Jan pulled her hand away. "Just go now, then."

"Subway, half an hour, meeting, one hour, I promise — at the most, subway back, half an hour. So you can be in your bed in the hotel room at precisely noon." He saluted.

Jan smiled. "Get out of here, you clown. I love you."

He about-faced and marched out of the room to the sound of Jan's muted laughter.

The subways were jammed with holiday shoppers but were running well and sure enough, a half hour later he was ringing Dot's doorbell. It was answered by her daughter Jeana.

The girl was tall as Bill had been, with pale skin and reddish hair. She was laughing at what someone behind her had just said and turned her head to see Peter standing there. She looked so happy Peter hadn't the heart to offer his condolences on her father's death, thus reminding her of the awful experience. What he took to be a girlfriend of hers was sitting on the stairs looking down at them. He smiled, introduced himself and was shown in to the kitchen where Dot was preparing coffee. Her son, Max, was sitting at the table eating breakfast in his pyjamas. Jeana went to join her friend.

"Max, could you give us some privacy?" Dot asked. "Peter is Eleanor's literary executor and is preparing her last book for publication. We have some details to discuss. Coffee, Peter?"

Peter took the same seat he'd used the last time he was there and watched Dot pour coffee as Max shambled from the room holding his cereal bowl.

"How is Annie?"

"Making a slow recovery. Thanks for asking. How are your kids coping?"

"With what?" As Peter's eyebrows lifted, she laughed and said, "Oh, you mean Bill's death. Well, it seems so long ago. Strange, eh? I'd say Max is having the more difficult time of it. Actually," she came to join him at the table, "that's what I want to talk to you about. Bill's death. The police have been questioning me again about some last-minute will Mum may have made. James Cooper says she phoned him to tell him that there was one — a holographic will, which is to say, a handwritten one — perfectly legal. She phoned him on the morning of the day she killed herself — I mean, was murdered. He says that Bill must have known about that will and that was why he killed her. But I think my mother would have told me if she was going to change her will. I mean, I was her daughter. And I would have respected her right to leave her money where she wanted to although I would have been surprised if she forgot Jeana and Max. So now the police think I was aware of the new will and they think I made Bill kill Mum to get our hands on the money. And they keep going over and over it until I think I may go crazy." She drank her coffee with trembling hands. "You didn't notice anything unusual when you went to the apartment, did you?"

Peter paused. "I told the police what I observed and I assure you it was nothing. Just that the scissors weren't in the kitchen, so I got some from Eleanor's desk. I don't think it means anything. And that my office at the university was burgled and a computer stolen a few weeks after I took possession of Eleanor's files."

"But that was kids, wasn't it? Trashing for the sake of it."

"Nothing was trashed. That's the strange thing. Just the computer taken and everything else searched. I really don't think it has anything to do with Eleanor. Or not with her death anyway." He paused again. "Do you trust Cooper? Could he be lying?"

"You think Cooper could have killed Mum? Oh, Peter, I never thought of that. Do you think we should tell the police?"

Peter replied hastily. "I'm sure the police have already considered the possibility. But it seems to me that if Bill killed Eleanor, then confessed and took his own life, the case should end there. Shouldn't it?"

Dot looked down at her hands holding the coffee cup. "They seem to think, the pathology report seems to suggest, that Bill was unconscious when he...that he didn't wrap himself in...that someone else did it."

"Good God. Someone in this house? Good God. But that's — "

"Me or the children," Dot finished his sentence grimly. "And the life insurance won't pay out as long as the police can't make up their minds. Suicide: no money. Murder: money."

"So it's in your interest to have Bill's death declared murder."

"As long as I didn't do it, yes."

"Dot, I have to go. No, really, I promised Jan I'd only stay an hour. I'll be in touch if I think of anything."

A troubled house, he thought as he jogged to the subway station. I am always relieved to leave there.

Christmas was hardly noticed by the DeWitt-Forrest parents that year, although Ruth surprised them by decorating the house with Jenny and Liza in their absence, buying gifts and filling stockings. The day itself was a quiet one with half the family in Toronto but Jan and Peter heard all about it from the excited girls on the telephone. Peter was glad to notice a little more show of affection coming from Annie as she convalesced in the hospital. Maybe her emotions were beginning to thaw from their previous state of indifference. Or maybe she was just entering a different stage of development. She was cleared to return home just before New Year's.

Peter's email inbox was loaded with two weeks' worth of correspondence and it was only in the lull following New Year's Day that he got to work catching up on it.

He'd let his human rights work slide and he tackled those messages first. One contained a file forwarded from a Chinese source: more documentation of Falun Gong members tortured or murdered. Two dreadful photos caught Peter's eye. The man had large burn marks all over the front of his body. Someone had turned him over and more marks were visible on the backs of his legs, but they were scars, not fresh wounds. Peter recognized those: he'd included seeing them when he wrote his police report. The dead face was visible in the first photo and Peter saw the blond hair, a little longer, with dark roots and, in the open mouth, a chipped front tooth.

PART 2

11

"So what are we going to do about Jenny?" Jan came into the study where Peter, untypically sitting at the desk, was taking a break from going through the author's proofs for Eleanor's book by flipping through a seed catalogue, and plunked herself down on the sofa.

He half turned to face her. "You mean the tantrums?"

"I mean everything. Her meanness to the other two; the fact that she can't be trusted around animals." She referred to Jenny's treatment of Marigold, Ruth's cat, the persecution of which culminated when Ruth narrowly prevented Jenny throwing the cat out Ruth's upstairs bathroom window. Apparently, and unbeknownst to Ruth, Jenny had been shampooing the cat, and, when it scratched and bit her, had resolved to punish it. Needless to say, Jenny was no longer welcome at Ruth's, though Ruth tried to remain affectionate to the child.

"I guess she needs counselling." Peter spoke reluctantly. He'd hoped their loving patience coupled with their "we're all in this together" philosophy would have helped Jenny get along. "Or we do," he added.

He sighed at the thought of adding another appointment to their already busy schedule. The two oldest girls were back at school. Annie had frequent follow-up appointments as well as the dialysis. He was due to start back to work in a week. Added to all of this was the freakish winter weather they had been experiencing — one- or two- or three-day blizzards followed by rain and the subsequent freeze-up. Conditions outside were treacherous, whether walking or driving, and every errand took extra time because of them. He rubbed his eyes and asked, "Are the services at least available out here?"

"If they're with a social worker, yes. If she refers us to a psychiatrist, it'll be in Toronto."

Peter groaned. "You've been talking to Dr. Stone?"

"Yeah. At Annie's last appointment."

Between them, Peter, Jan and Dr. Stone had come up with several explanations for Annie's condition. She was a lucky, wanted child in China who received a transplant, then became an orphan. The darker scenario: that she was first an organ donor, then a test subject receiving a kidney as part of a study to see how long people lived when weaned off of immunosuppressant drugs. But how she had become part of an adoption, or whether she'd been substituted for the child originally intended for the DeWitt-Forrest family, they suspected they'd never know.

Jan continued, "So, we go for it?"

"I suppose. We have to do something."

"What are you working on now?" She came over to look at the proofs. "Oh, Eleanor's book. Will you be glad when it's published? Stupid question. Of course you will. What I mean to say, and I know it's selfish of me, is, after, will you have more time?"

"I'm not sure," Peter replied slowly. "The publisher wants me to do some readings, promote the book. Because of the political angle, he thinks it could arouse more interest than poetry books usually do. I think it'll be local: Kingston, Montreal, Ottawa — Toronto certainly. I don't know where else." He put his arms around her waist. "Have I been holing up in here too much?"

"You have, a bit. And if you're not doing Eleanor work then you're doing China work. Don't get me wrong. I think it's wonderful and I'm proud of you for getting involved. But we have three kids right here and one of them is a bit disturbed. All three need as much attention as we can muster, between the two of us." She sat down on the sofa, clasped hands pressed between her knees, and looked at the floor. "I know you earn all the money…" Her voice trailed off. "I wish I could help."

"Is this about money?" Peter moved to sit next to her. "Because we have enough, Jan. Are you tired of staying home with the girls?"

"No! I love it. It's just what I always wanted. I just feel bad not earning anything." Jan had made decent money working as an interior designer for an architectural firm before they'd met and plunged into home ownership, marriage and child rearing.

"I'll try to say 'no' more often to the China work or do it at the office and leave it there. Would that help? It sounds as if you need me to be more available when I'm home."

"Yes and yes." She smiled. "Thanks." Then, after a pause, "But what happened about your friend in China? What was his name?"

"Xhu Xi. Chu Hsi by the old spelling and easier to pronounce. Yeah, it was him, poor guy. Turns out he was gay and a journalist. Not a member of Falun Gong. Just trying to report what he found out about human rights abuses. He was detained a few years ago and tortured — I saw the scars when we met in China — but was friends with some influential people so they arranged his release. The first time. He wasn't so lucky the second. And you know what's funny?" He brought the laptop over. "I googled his name. Look. Chu Hsi was a twelfth-century Chinese philosopher who refused promotion and stayed a humble teacher. He hated factions and was unhappy with the kind of people who came to power. He used to write letters to the emperor stating his views and opinions."

"A dissident," said Jan.

"Certainly a dissenting voice in his time," added Peter. "So we don't know our man's real name but he picked a great pseudonym."

"All honour to him," said Jan in a low voice.

"All honour," echoed Peter.

Jenny had her assessment from a social worker who did indeed recommend they seek counselling. Their choice was either to drive to Toronto for psychiatry at the children's hospital, which would be covered by the health care system, or try their luck with a local psychologist — and pay. As the hospital was booking appointments eight months in the future, they opted for the private psychologist. So when the call came from Jenny's school that she was bullying the other kids, they could claim to already be working on a solution.

Peter remarked when they made their decision, "As long as the care is comparable, think of the money for the psychologist as going for the appointment and not on gas and a meal on the way if we were going to Toronto for free treatment. It works out to almost the same amount."

They arranged to go every other week and, according to the wishes of Dr. Whiteside, a thin, youngish woman who projected a calm competency, sometimes one or both parents sat in on the sessions, sometimes neither. After the first few sessions she phoned to let them know what she thought was going on. She spoke to Jan.

"The social misconduct can be worked on: reinforcing good behaviour, gentle punishments for bad, but there's evidence of PTSD, post-traumatic stress disorder, and that's going to be trickier to deal with: some bad experience or experiences in early life. She was two when you adopted her. Much may have occurred up to that point. Now that she's older she may be able to articulate some of that." She added encouragingly, "We'll get there."

As Jan told Peter that night, "She said we have to be alert to clues in what Jenny may do or say as to what this past experience might have been."

"Probably just being in an orphanage would be enough to leave some scars. How many more appointments does she think she'll need?"

"You know they never say that. We have to be patient and hope there's a breakthrough. Meanwhile, Liza's birthday is coming up. Thoughts?"

They celebrated Liza's fourth birthday with the same type of party they'd had for Jenny, minus the screaming. Four little girls from preschool arrived the last Sunday afternoon in February, carried through deep snow from their cars to the house, played pin-the-tail-on-the-donkey and musical chairs, ate birthday cake, and watched Liza open presents. Jenny was good and even Annie seemed to enjoy herself, trying to keep up with the older children. The birthday girl, Liza, usually content to live in Jenny's shadow, blossomed at the attention, asserting herself during the games, but pleasantly.

March brought steadier weather: fewer storms, longer, sunnier days and, as usual, Peter felt his spirits lift. He started some of his seeds for the garden indoors under lights in the basement: the plants that could go in the ground early in May, such as broccoli and cabbage, and the ones that would be planted in early June but that needed a long indoor growing time, such as eggplant and basil. He realized he hadn't given much thought to Eleanor's and Bill's deaths lately and wondered what the status of their cases was. He emailed Smythe and was invited to a "discussion" with the policeman.

"Uh-oh," he remarked to Jan. "I should have left well enough alone."

"Well, here we are," remarked Peter, placing his hands on the table. "Now what?" He looked around the restaurant: not many people eating chicken at three o'clock of a Tuesday afternoon.

"Now you tell me what possible connection you think may exist between the deaths of your friend Eleanor Brandon and her son-in-law Bill Hyde."

"Are you asking for my help?"

"The police are always asking for the public's help. Not that we usually get it. I'm asking for an informal discussion where we brainstorm. You bring your knowledge, both past and present, of the people involved. I bring access to information and the ability to make and prove a case."

The waitress brought coffee and took their order.

"Where's Smith?"

"We find that it's better in informal discussions to just meet one on one."

"So no record?"

"I'm going to make my usual notes." Smythe brought out the by-now-familiar notebook.

"Do you have a whole pile of those things at home?"

"I find blue a soothing colour and like the continuity using the same format provides. And, yes, I bought a box of them cheap at a yard sale."

"So, I'll begin with Eleanor."

"What was she like?"

They both straightened as the waitress put their apple pie in front of them and topped up their coffee.

"She was tough. She faced things. She made decisions. It was she who ended our relationship. She said I had a lot of growing to do — which was true — and that she needed to do her work without distraction. I suppose she was right. I wasn't in love with her, just flattered and stimulated by the attention of this lovely, intelligent woman. I got the impression at the time that she didn't want too much emotional responsibility. Her divorce had hit her hard though I don't know if there had been any scandal. I would have been a kid at the time, like Dot."

"Do you get any feeling of resentment toward her mother when you speak with Dorothy Brandon-Hyde?"

"None. She just wished that if her mother had changed her will and disinherited her that she would have left something for the grandkids Jeana and Max Brandon-Hyde. Moot point because no will disinheriting Dot has been found. Other reasons to suspect Dot?"

"Money is a powerful motivator. We've gone into Bill Hyde's financial situation in some depth and if he had any resources, they were well hidden. If his wife knew he was broke and was running out of money herself...she seems like someone who likes her home and her comforts. What if all that was threatened — first by a spendthrift husband and second by a mother who took her politics more seriously than family responsibilities? Her children are at the most expensive time of their lives. Both will presumably go to university. The son plays hockey. Those are big expenses."

"What about the income from her trust fund?"

"Well, those investments took a hit in 2008 though they're recovering now. Her husband was managing her assets at that time. She moved them elsewhere after his malfeasance at work was discovered. He must have resented that."

"So she had experience of trusting him, losing money and ceasing to trust him, at least financially." Peter signalled to the waitress for more coffee.

"And trust funds only go so far when you're up against inflation, rising city taxes, maintenance of a large home."

"Okay, I get it. Money is the obvious motivator for Dot. Anything else?"

Smythe looked directly at Peter. "Yes. After money comes sex or love or whatever it is that makes people commit murders. One theory, and Smith likes this one a lot, is that you and Mrs. Brandon-Hyde were or are lovers or that one of you would so like to be."

Peter pursed his lips with distaste. "I see. I can't help you with this. You're on your own. But go ahead."

"So this would mean you conspired to murder both Eleanor Brandon and Bill Hyde: the one to prevent her from giving away the money you'd need, the other as he was a physical impediment to you being with his wife."

"And does this scenario include me killing my wife and kids and hoping to get away with it? And then living happily ever after with Dot?"

"You say you were at work in your university office at the time of Eleanor's death, but that's not easily proved or disproved. And you could have easily driven from Dunbarton to Toronto, been let into the Brandon-Hyde home by either Dorothy or Bill Hyde, murdered him and driven back to Dunbarton in what? Four hours?"

"You're not seriously suggesting this, are you?"

"I'm not, but that's not to say all of it is untrue. Even if you are wholly innocent, it doesn't mean that Dorothy Brandon-Hyde doesn't have feelings for you that may have motivated her to kill."

"But that's ridiculous. I hadn't seen her for twenty years until at her mother's funeral. No, it makes no sense."

"I agree, although she could have conceived a sudden passion for you there which led to her murdering her husband." Smythe smiled. Peter sensed him considering his stocky figure, greying and thinning hair, and the wrinkles that worry about Annie had deepened. "Maybe not. So let's move on to supposing you as the sole murderer working alone."

Peter flung himself back in the booth. "There's more of this shit?"

"Let's just get it out in the open, shall we? One theory is that you killed Eleanor because you knew you were going to be her literary executor and your career, your publishing career, has been in a slump. You'd write a book or two, make a lot of money and get back on track. Why are you smiling?"

"Do you know how much money Canadian editors or even authors make? And it's not as if Eleanor was such a high-profile poet/activist that the whole world would care enough to read her poems or any biography that might follow."

"Are you going to write a biography?"

"I might." Peter paused as Smythe's eyebrows rose. "I might, but my wife has recently requested that I take on fewer projects and participate more in our family life, so any biography I might write would have to be done over a long period of time. Again, little money to be made compared to the hours of work that are involved. And why would I then have killed Bill?"

"He found out somehow. Maybe he tried to blackmail you. Or he thought you wanted his wife and threatened you himself. The point is that both victims knew you and would probably have opened their doors to you."

"Are we done? Because I'd like to discuss other suspects, if you don't mind."

Smythe smiled. "It's not nice being suspected, is it? All of the above is supposition and doesn't get us far. So let's look at Bill Hyde. We like him for the Eleanor murder because of the money angle mostly. He might have lost his family if Eleanor had changed her will. Dorothy could have figured he was a liability, not an asset, and divorced him."

"What if Eleanor knew something about him, knew something that his partners couldn't forgive, that might send him to prison?"

"Back to blackmail. Only Eleanor's doing it to him and it's emotional. And again, he might lose his family if she told Dorothy and he caused another scandal. It's interesting." Smythe made a note. "We think that if he did kill his mother-in-law, it's a possibility that his wife knew, either before or after the fact. If before, she may have urged him to do it. If after, she may have colluded in protecting him until such time as she decided he was expendable or a danger to her."

"How do you mean?"

"Well, we're assuming Hyde loved his wife. What if he didn't? Wouldn't he get her money if she died? Maybe Dorothy killed him — a pre-emptive strike, if you like?"

"I find the idea of either of these people — Dot or Bill — strangling and asphyxiating Eleanor grotesque. I can't quite see Dot doing something to Bill, even if he was already passed out from alcohol."

Smythe interrupted. "The autopsy didn't find any marks of violence on the body."

"You mean no thumb or finger marks on the neck or throat?"

"Exactly. So whoever did it, didn't need to use force and may be a small person."

"Like Dot. But then leaving him for one of their kids to find?"

"Maybe that was an accident. Maybe she meant to 'find' him but the daughter turned up at home early. And either of the two kids could have found him passed out and taped the bag over his head. Believe me, children can loathe a parent enough to kill. Not often. But it happens."

Peter thought of Max Brandon-Hyde's evident misery and his sister's persistent liveliness.

There was a pause as both men looked down at the table. Peter broke the silence first. "You got kids?"

"No."

"I'm trying to imagine me killing my parents or my children killing me. It's quite difficult."

"Sometimes children feel so much antipathy to one parent and so much loyalty to the other that they do extraordinary things. The alibis are vague and hard to disprove. The daughter was at her friend's house and chose to walk home. Dorothy was picking up her son from hockey practice."

"Oh."

"What?"

"Well, when I was there the first time, for dinner, she said the hockey coach usually brought the boys home — or at least brought Max home."

"The boy says she brought him home."

"So that's what you meant."

"What?"

"When you spoke of loyalty to one parent. You think one or both of the kids may be lying to protect Dot."

"It's complicated. The coach confirms that the night Bill Hyde died, he didn't drive Max Brandon-Hyde home. The boy said his mother was picking him up. She may have been using the kids. She killed Bill, went to get Max to distance herself from the crime scene and planned to discover Bill's 'suicide' herself sometime that evening."

Peter rose and went to use the bathroom. When he returned he was surprised to find Smythe paying at the cash. Obviously they were done. They stepped out into Toronto's rush hour.

"What did that accomplish?" Peter asked.

"It let me gauge your reactions to various scenarios. It gave me more information of the possible dynamics at play within the Brandon-Hyde household. I don't actually view you as a suspect, Mr. Forrest, but I need you to keep me informed about any further meetings you may have with Dorothy Brandon-Hyde or her lawyer. It all helps to build up character profiles and understand motives. Are you with me?"

"I came today, didn't I? I want to know why Eleanor died and whether her family was involved."

Smythe gave him a look. "Be seeing you," he said and walked away.

12

Peter peeled off the pink and silver polka-dotted foil and popped the little chocolate egg into his mouth. There was a satisfying combination of muddy smells and the sound of running water as accumulated snow melted in nearby fields and soil softened. He tilted his head back and squinted, looking up at the noisy passing of geese.

Jan had hidden half the Easter eggs in the house the night before. Peter had just finished the outside. The routine was: inside hunt, breakfast (boiled eggs of course), outside hunt. As he went inside he could tell by the girls' squeals that they were already on the move. Well, Jenny and Liza were. Jan was in the bathroom getting Annie ready. She called down the stairs, "Supervise those other two, would you? Make sure they don't find all the eggs before Annie comes."

"Don't worry."

Jan brought Annie downstairs.

"Here, give her to me." He held Annie while turning and silently showing Jan the cache of eggs in his jacket pocket. He wiggled his eyebrows up and down, secret spy style. "We're good."

As Jan went to boil eggs and make toast, he showed Annie what the other two were up to. They each had a little basket of different coloured strips of paper woven together that they'd made with Ruth the weekend before and were tearing around announcing each find before plopping the eggs in the baskets. "Where's Annie's basket, kids?" They paid him no attention at all.

Annie pointed to the fireplace mantelpiece.

"There it is. I wonder if the Easter bunny left anything for you." He walked over to the mantel and let Annie look into and then grasp her basket. She struggled to get down so he followed her around, planting eggs, then drawing her attention to them by saying things like "Did you look over there, Annie?" and "Now, how did Jenny and Liza miss that one?" By the time his pocket was empty, Annie had made quite a haul and Jan was calling them for breakfast.

As they ate, the girls talked about how many eggs they had collected and how many more they'd find outside. They spilled their baskets onto the table and counted. If a bit more chocolate egg than chicken egg was consumed, Jan and Peter didn't mind. Then it was upstairs to dress and outside for more hunting. Peter helped Annie by carrying her so she spotted all the eggs he'd hidden up high.

After the hunt, Jan confiscated all three baskets, saying they could have some more chocolate after lunch. Then she told all three to go and play.

"That was fun," grinned Peter, pouring them each a cup of coffee.

"So far, so good," Jan replied. That and "one day at a time" had become their words to live by since Jenny's and Annie's problems had become preoccupations.

Jenny seemed to be responding to counselling. At least there hadn't been any more warning calls from school, and twice Ruth had let her visit Marigold, feed and brush the cat, hoping she'd develop a little empathy toward a fellow creature.

Annie's health was pretty good, considering all she was going through. Since her illness at Christmas she'd been sleeping on a little low bed near a window in Jan and Peter's big bedroom. But Jan thought it was time she returned to her own room, and that led to talk of reorganizing the sleeping arrangements. Jenny was offered her own room while Liza and Annie would share. Today was the day Peter and Jan had set aside to shift the girls' things.

"Right. I'll move Jenny's stuff into Annie's old room first, then put Annie's stuff in with Liza."

The work didn't take long and Peter was just rearranging Jenny's artwork on the walls of her new room when she appeared in the doorway.

"Hello. What do you think of your new room?"

"It's okay." She entered and looked around at her things, lay down on the bed and shut her eyes.

Peter sat next to her and rubbed her leg. "Tired?" he asked.

She kicked her leg at him and turned to face the wall. "No."

He took a deep breath and left her. He finished moving Annie in with Liza, made a list of a few things he thought the rooms now needed — a rug for Jenny, a reading lamp for Liza — called Jenny to lunch and went downstairs.

"All done?" asked Jan.

"Oh, boy, hot dogs!" he said, smiling at Liza and Annie and then at Jenny as she stomped into the room. "Yeah, but I need a few things. I thought I'd take a drive to the furniture store. Do we all want to go?"

"I'll let you do that," said Jan. "I'll hang out here and wait for Mum to arrive."

"Jenny, do you want to come with me?" Peter asked gently. "You could pick out a rug for your room."

Jenny looked interested. "All right," she said.

The drive to the nearest big furniture/hardware store took half an hour and then they took their time making selections: a bold orange, green and beige rug for Jenny; a pink and white touch-on lamp for Liza; and, so she wouldn't feel left out, a package of peel-and-stick balloons Peter imagined would look good floating on the wall next to Annie's bed. By the time they were done it was almost suppertime.

Jenny dozed on the way home. The hours away from the others seemed to have helped. Peter made a mental note to set aside a little more time for her.

When they got home Ruth was there with a big dish of scalloped potatoes and three soft, brown toy bunnies wearing T-shirts that said "Chocolate Bunny" on them. The ham was done and maple-glazed carrots were finishing in the oven. The house smelled terrific.

After the big meal, the girls went to watch TV while the adults lingered over their wine. Peter commented, "I think Jenny responded well to having some quiet time with just me. I'll try to do that more often."

Ruth responded, "I'll take her on her own, if that's what she needs. Maybe she's an introvert and gets overstimulated easily." She finished her wine. "Better have a coffee if I'm going to drive home."

"Oh, just stay, Mum." Jan poured her mother another glass. "The cat will be fine. And the spare room is ready." She looked at Peter. "It is ready, isn't it?"

"I didn't go in there," he replied. "Which reminds me, I've got to get the rug and other stuff from the car."

He went outside and breathed the cool, damp air. He could hear a few early frogs beginning their clucking in a nearby creek. "Peter," Jan called, "telephone." He cursed quietly as she handed him the portable. He sat on the front steps. "Hello?"

"James Cooper here. Happy Easter. Sorry to disturb but I wonder if we could take a meeting this week?"

"Happy Easter. Yes. This week? Tuesday would be fine. See you at ten? At your office." Peter disconnected and looked up at the stars. He hummed "back to life, back to reality" and went inside with his purchases.

As Jan settled the girls into their new sleeping arrangements, he placed the rug next to Jenny's bed. She stroked its softness before climbing between the sheets. Liza turned her new lamp on and off at least a dozen times while Annie traced the outline of her new balloons with her fingers.

"Well done," murmured Jan as they went downstairs to rejoin Ruth.

That night Jenny had a nightmare that woke everyone in the house. As Jan and Ruth calmed the other girls, Peter held Jenny as she sobbed over and over, "Don't put me in the room, Daddy. Don't put me in the room."

She slept in Jan and Peter's bed that night and the next day, Easter Monday, he moved her furniture back into the room she had shared with Liza. He placed the new rug between the two beds and moved Annie into her own room, peeling the floating balloons from one room's wall, resticking them in the other.

"A breakthrough, do you think?" asked Jan that night after the tired girls had gone peacefully to bed.

"I would say so," replied Peter grimly. "For sure tell Dr. Whiteside. Traffic will be terrible tomorrow morning. I'll have to leave early. I'd better get some sleep. Coming?"

"Soon. I'd like to read for a bit. See you later."

He was soon asleep.

He could hear a baby crying. The door of a room was slightly ajar and he was walking toward it. Yet every time he got near the doorway something distracted him and he had to move away, only to find himself approaching the open door and the crying baby again. He felt frustrated and afraid. If he could just get inside the room… He jerked awake as Jan slid into bed.

"Bad dream," he muttered into her neck.

"Not you too."

"Better now you're here."

A fine rain was falling as Peter parked and walked the short distance to Cooper's building. It looked the same except the importer had closed and brown paper was pasted all over the inside of the ground floor showroom's windows. Someone had papered the outside of the windows with posters for a local band. Peter doubted Cooper appreciated the counterculture using his building to advertise.

He was a bit early — traffic hadn't been so bad — but decided to go up anyway and was greeted by a different receptionist, an Asian woman this time. As had been the case the last time he visited, they had the waiting area to themselves. He was beginning to doubt the existence of Cooper's associates when the phone on the receptionist's desk buzzed and she motioned him to go through. As he rose, another man, middle-aged, Chinese, came out of one of the other offices, seemed surprised to see Peter and exchanged comments with the receptionist in Mandarin.

Cooper rose from behind the same shining table and offered coffee or tea. Peter accepted tea and the receptionist soon arrived with a tray while he and Cooper were exchanging the usual pleasantries.

Cooper seemed especially interested to hear about Annie's condition, her boredom and discomfort during dialysis, the wait time for a kidney transplant. Peter was surprised, as he hadn't counted compassion among the lawyer's attributes.

"So bring me up to speed with your book of Eleanor's poems," Cooper said, offering a plate of cookies.

Peter took one. "Well, as I indicated to you by email, the book is published and has been placed in the usual marketplaces. I'm due to do some book signings in various stores over the next couple of months. And then we'll just have to wait for reviews and the first sales figures." He ate and sipped. "I'm thinking I would like to write about Eleanor's life but I can't promise to be quick about it."

"My understanding is that biographies often take a long time to complete, if they're comprehensive," the lawyer interjected.

"Yes. I'd have to do interviews with those who knew Eleanor as well as comb archives for her early life history. I do have a sabbatical year coming up and would probably work on the book then."

"That seems satisfactory," said the lawyer.

"Was there something else you wanted to discuss?" Peter ventured. "There really haven't been any expenses to the estate. And you and Dot agreed that any royalty payments from the poems would go to human rights organizations as per Eleanor's wishes."

The lawyer got up and looked out the window at the grey day. They could hear the rain drizzling and dripping from the eaves. He turned and spoke.

"Forrest, I have in fact read your book and I'm concerned by some of the content in your introduction to Eleanor's work."

"Like what?"

"You allege the torture and imprisonment of Falun Gong members in China is linked to live organ harvesting."

"It is," Peter replied bluntly.

"Let me continue. And then you mention some western pharmaceutical companies who manufacture and test immunosuppressive drugs in China as having an 'I don't want to know about it' policy."

"They don't want to know," said Peter, steadily looking at Cooper. "Why do you care?"

"I care because you are damaging the reputation of my clients, the Brandon family, involving yourself and them in possible future litigation."

"Everything in my introduction has been verified and footnoted. I give copious references at the end of the book." He paused. "Including referencing Eleanor herself. Furthermore, any biography I might in future write would go into these matters in even greater depth. How else explain some of the poems that deal with disappeared family members and unidentified and brutalized bodies?"

"Those poems are products of Eleanor's imagination and the fact that you take them as factual representations is one of the reasons that I cannot support you as the right author of an official biography of Eleanor — and I will so advise Dot."

Peter got up to leave. The lawyer continued.

"And, on a personal note, Forrest, you might want to be careful who you piss off in the pharmaceutical business. It sounds like your daughter is going to need all the help she can get." Cooper's eyes narrowed. "It would be a shame if her name got bumped lower down the list of future kidney recipients."

Peter froze in shock, then replied coldly, "I don't believe you have any way to control that list and you should be careful making threats that concern a member of my family. Don't think I won't tell Dot about this conversation and that I refuse to have any further contact with you. I believe I'll also tell the police."

"Your word against mine, Forrest. Your word against mine."

Peter was vibrating as he got into his car and during the minutes it took him to calm himself he wrote down as much of the conversation as he could remember. Once he'd arrived at work he sent one email to both Dorothy and to Smythe. After that he felt better and got busy marking essays and assigning grades.

Checking his inbox before he left, he saw Smythe had answered his message with a brief "Interesting. Later." There was no response from Dot.

13

"Dot's bound to take Cooper's advice. She's known him all her life." Peter and Jan were sitting at the kitchen table after supper.

"She's an intelligent woman. She'll think for herself. So you definitely want to do the bio then?"

"Only if I'm on sabbatical. How dare he threaten me about speaking about Western pharmaceutical companies' activities in China? How dare he sneer about Annie's condition? What a bastard!"

"Peter, calm down. He must have an agenda. Maybe he works for one of those companies and has a conflict of interest."

"Then he has the problem, not me. I'm going to phone Dot. The book tour starts soon and I need to know how she feels about this."

Peter went into the study and dialled Dot's number. She picked up the phone almost immediately.

"Peter. I'm glad you've called. I just spoke with James. He's very upset."

"Hello, Dot. Did he tell you he threatened me? That if I continue to speak against Chinese repression of Falun Gong, he would fix it so Annie would be moved to the bottom of the organ recipient list?"

"Peter, he can't mean it." She sounded aghast. "He told me you were going to blow the Chinese dissident part of Mum's work all out of proportion to the literary merit of her poems. And he advised me to terminate your work as literary executor."

"Dot, what I discuss in the introduction to the book as well as what I'll discuss at any speaking events is at least two-thirds Eleanor's life and literary output and one-third her politics. She only came to activism in the last twenty years of her life, right?"

"Right. So you're arguing you'll keep a sense of proportion. James doesn't seem to think you will."

"He doesn't understand that the poems of dissidence Eleanor was writing herself, as well as those by Chinese dissidents, are symptoms of a greater evil being perpetuated not just by the Chinese government but by individuals and companies outside of China."

There was a moment's pause then Dot spoke.

"You seem very wrought up by it all, Peter."

"My daughter may have been involved in organ trafficking in some way. We don't know. She wasn't the child we were scheduled to adopt. It's been a hell of a year."

"I hear you. Here, too. Listen, there's something you should know. Bill used to make my investments. It just made sense, as he was in the financial industry."

"I know. The police told me. And after 2008, when he got caught cheating, you transferred them elsewhere."

"Well, most of them. Bill swore the pharmaceutical stocks would never lose value, said James recommended them to him. So I let him continue to manage those. And he was right. They lost value but compared to other stocks, not so much. I told Mum and she thought two of the companies sounded familiar. Sure enough, after she checked, she told me they were considered unethical investments because of their collusion within the field of transplant medicine in China. Something about condemned prisoners being forced to donate their organs."

Peter let out his breath. "So what did you do?"

"I told Bill to get rid of the stock and he did. I suppose James liked the returns and kept his. Peter, I have to think about all this.

But go ahead with the promotion of Mum's book. I trust you to be prudent where her literary interests lie."

"Thank you, Dot. I appreciate it."

Over the next month and a half, Peter made a few quick trips to the major cities of central Canada, flying where possible so as not to be away from home for more than a couple of days at a time. One trip took in Hamilton, Kitchener-Waterloo and London; another Montreal and Ottawa. Toronto and outlying area events as well as one in Kingston could be managed by car, and he would generally be home the same night.

He enjoyed presenting the poems. Sometimes, at readings, he was one of three or four authors from the same publishing house. It was always interesting to observe how others presented their material. At other events, say, book signings at bookstores, he was usually the sole presenter. These occasions involved chatting directly with the public as he sat at a table near the door, with what he hoped was an inviting expression on his face.

One such afternoon he looked up to see a young Chinese man approaching with a copy of the book. But instead of handing the book to Peter to sign, the man, possibly a student, held the book up and, looking around at the other customers, said in a loud voice, "This book is full of lies."

Peter replied evenly, "What do you mean?"

The man continued. "This book says Falun Gong are peaceful people. The Chinese government tells us they are members of a harmful cult, disobedient to the good of the people of China. This book says Falun Gong are prisoners and doctors take their organs for wealthy Westerners. The Chinese government would not permit this. China has the best organ transplantation system in the world. No wonder Westerners as well as Chinese can get transplants there. Faster and better than outside China."

Customers edged away from the man until he was alone facing Peter. The store manager came over. "I'm afraid I have to ask you to leave, sir," she said to the man.

"Why? I only speak the truth. Why don't you answer me?" he asked Peter.

Peter said nothing. He wasn't going to argue. That's what the fellow wanted. Eventually, he left.

"Oh dear," said the manager.

"Never mind," Peter said thoughtfully. "People can decide for themselves. Thank you for asking him to leave."

On the drive home that evening, Peter wondered what else might happen now the book was in circulation. Not much, he concluded. It was still poetry with poetry's small audience; never mind the author's or editor's politics.

He was wrong.

When he got home, an irate Jan was waiting.

"Listen to this." She turned on the phone answer service playback.

"Peter Forrest, you are a liar and an enemy of the Chinese people. Do you think about death? Are you afraid to die? You have children. Don't you want them to be safe?" On and on it went, interspersed with the clicks made when an angry Jan interrupted the calls.

"All day, Peter. I suppose we'll have to change our number, be unlisted. That'll be a gigantic headache. And I know who'll have to deal with it. Me. I'll have to call all our contacts and friends, all the agencies we deal with for the girls."

"Why do you assume I won't help, Jan? I'll call the police right now and get them to try and trace the caller, for a start. Don't delete the messages, okay?"

"Well, obviously don't delete the messages." The sound of crying coming from upstairs distracted her.

Seizing his chance, Peter said, "I'll go."

"Hello, Annie." He lifted her out of her bed and sat in the rocking chair. "Are you okay?" She quieted and he cuddled her for a few minutes, then went down to make his peace with Jan.

When the phone messages were analyzed by the police, they were traced to a cellphone registered in a false name at a real address. The people there claimed to know nothing about it. Meanwhile, Jan and Peter had received anti–Falun Gong literature and threats in the mail. Peter's book tour was almost concluded, but just in case, Smith and Smythe attended the last two events, both held in Toronto on the same day. Nothing happened at either. While he was grateful for their interest, it amused Peter to watch a grim-faced Smith keeping an eye on the mostly middle-aged or elderly poetry lovers who attended.

After the second event, Smith requested a meeting and Peter, thinking they were wrapping up business to do with his family's harassment, agreed. Instead of a restaurant, however, they returned to the police station and entered a small conference room.

"Oh," said Peter.

Macdonald was sitting in a comfortable padded swivel chair at one end of the long table and he rose to shake hands with Peter, who found himself repeating the same words he'd used when first meeting the man in China. "Am I in trouble?"

Smith cleared his throat. "What this is, Mr. Forrest, is an informal discussion, hopefully in all our interests. We are interested in solving two Toronto murders. Mr. Macdonald—" Smith paused and flicked Macdonald a look. "Mr. Macdonald has a wider brief, as I'm sure you've gathered. And convergence between our two departments has occurred in the person of James Cooper, lawyer for Eleanor Brandon, deceased, and Bill Hyde, also deceased."

"Mr. Forrest, my name is Ross Macdonald and I'm an S.L.O., a security liaison officer, working, as you know, at the Canadian consulate in Shanghai."

"Yes."

"My job there is to collect information as it pertains to assessing prospective immigrants to Canada."

Peter felt his face grow tight. "Yes," he repeated, in what he thought was a calm voice.

"I am following up on a file that was brought to my attention in June of last year." He looked down at a paper on the desk. "June 7th, to be precise."

Peter looked over at Smythe, conspicuously not taking notes but fiddling with his pen as he stared down at the surface of the table.

Macdonald continued. "A discrepancy noticed by a clerk between the photograph of your daughter and her actual appearance."

Peter said nothing. The pause lengthened. Surprisingly, it was Smith who broke the silence. "Come on, Macdonald, cut the crap. Get to the point."

Macdonald referred to another paper in the file in front of him. "I have learned from reading your report of your China trip made to the Toronto police that when you visited your daughter's orphanage June 3rd you witnessed two occurrences that you didn't mention to me when we met in Shanghai. One, the medical van behind the military building. Two, a surgical team ostensibly working in the basement of the orphanage. Why is that?"

"At the time I didn't register what I had seen as anything out of the ordinary. I didn't think medical van, I just thought van. And I assumed the doctors were operating on the kids, but for their good, not to hurt them, as they may have been. Then, later, after I got home and researched Falun Gong persecution, I thought them suspicious and included them in my report."

"Mmm." Macdonald rearranged some of his papers. "Are you aware, Mr. Forrest, of the penalties for human trafficking, for knowingly substituting one child for another and taking her across international boundaries?"

Peter kept silent. What did this guy want?

"Falun Gong, Mr. Forrest," Macdonald continued. "Do you believe everything you read about Falun Gong?"

"There are some very well-reasoned and factually supported arguments that suggest they have been brutally persecuted by the Chinese government," Peter replied woodenly.

"Mmm." Macdonald pushed a photograph across the table. "Recognize him?"

Peter picked it up. A middle-aged Chinese man. "No."

"How about him?" Another middle-aged Chinese man. "No."

"How about her?" This photo was of a young Asian woman.

"Yes, I think...I think she's James Cooper's receptionist."

"Ah," said Macdonald, making a note. "Would you like to look at the photos of the men again, please?"

Peter looked. "This one." He pushed the picture at Macdonald. "At Cooper's office. Spoke to her." He gestured at the woman's picture.

Macdonald gathered the photos into a neat pile, paper-clipped them and made another note. Another photo was pushed across the table. Peter winced.

"That's the man who gave me the USB in Shanghai." The photo showed Chu Hsi alive, posing with some friends at what looked like a picnic in a park.

"And why did you accept and bring out the information this man gave you?"

"After I viewed the file, I thought it was important it be seen. In the West."

"And were you, at that time, an activist, Mr. Forrest?"

"You know I wasn't." Peter was angry. He turned to Smith and Smythe. "I bet I know who stole my computer at the university. This guy or his buddies, checking up on Eleanor after her death, closing her file." He gestured with contempt at the file that lay on the table. "But you probably knew that, didn't you?"

Smythe made a calming gesture with his hand, indicating Peter should settle down.

Peter chose to continue. He readdressed Macdonald. "Have you read your mandate lately? CSIS is barred from investigating 'lawful advocacy, protest or dissent.'"

"You're assuming I work for CSIS. In any case, the practice of Falun Gong is outlawed in China and Canada must respect the laws of foreign countries."

"Except where human rights violations and crimes against humanity are suspected," Peter shot back.

"Hey!" Smith interjected. "This isn't the United Nations. Let's get back to the case. Forrest, we think Cooper or someone known to him killed both Eleanor Brandon and Bill Hyde. Cooper's implicated in a Canadian-Chinese syndicate organizing transplant tourism. If one or both of the victims were going to blow the whistle on him, he'd lose his position and much of his income. Macdonald here would be happy if we nailed the jerk on murder charges and kept the whole other business out of the news." He looked at Macdonald with disgust. "For political reasons."

"Are you sure Cooper's involved?" asked Peter.

"Oh, he's involved," replied Macdonald. "His latest receptionist, the one in the picture, works for us. She's given us all his contacts: the doctors here and the nurses at dialysis units who refer patients to Cooper. There's a travel agency involved."

"So you do want to shut them down?" Peter knew his voice reflected the bewilderment he was feeling.

Macdonald snapped, "Of course we want to shut them down. They're not breaking the law by brokering organ transplants or making travel arrangements, but Cooper and other Canadians are perpetrating tax fraud if nothing else and he consults with several multinational pharmaceutical companies with ties to China. He introduces them to the right hospitals, doctors and officials in China — the ones who'll accept bribes — so they can conduct business there. They don't want to be linked to some sleazy Canadian lawyer who's murdering people who've found out about one of his lucrative sidelines."

Peter spoke bitterly. "So we get him for the murders but conceal the Chinese angle to protect those companies?"

"Most of it." Macdonald sighed. "Look, I'm just the errand boy here. I'm sorry about your kid. But we want to catch him red-handed and — "

Peter slowly finished the sentence. "And I have a kid who needs a kidney."

"That's it. And, in return, the red flag that popped up at the Shanghai consulate when you arrived with a different kid will disappear. Permanently."

"My wife can't know. What am I saying? Of course, she'll have to know. Oh, God!" Peter exhaled forcefully. "All right. I'll call when I'm ready."

The interview with police and security was nowhere near as scary as the one Peter had with Jan when he got home that night.

"Are you kidding me, Peter? You're going to star in a sting operation and catch an international human organ trafficker?"

"He doesn't traffic in organs. Well, I suppose he does, actually. No. He brokers the deals, brings the recipient to the donor. I don't think he deals with the donors or the doctors who do the harvesting. They're mostly contacted by the hospitals where the transplant occurs. That's who he deals with — those administrators and doctors. It's all those distinctions that I'm going to try to find out. With your permission."

"With my permission? Peter, this whole thing has been a nightmare since you brought Annie home. The calls, the letters, the meetings with police. It's bizarre. I want my quiet life back."

"So, listen, if I can get Cooper, it all goes away. Annie's record of not being Annie is expunged, and we never have to worry about the government forcing us to return her to China. The Brandon-Hyde family gets to find out who murdered two of their relatives and the case is closed. I'll go on sabbatical next year and we'll relax. I promise. But I have to do this. I need to do this."

"Will Annie have to be involved?" Jan asked in a small voice.

"I don't know. Maybe a little."

"Oh my God, Peter!"

"What? It'll be fine. I'll be right there. Do you want to come?"

"I wouldn't be able to control myself!"

"All right. Me and Annie. Finishing what we started."

In May Annie turned two. Almost a year since she'd come to them. They kept the celebration low-key—just them and Ruth. Peter watched as Jan brought in the birthday cake: only two candles with one extra for good luck. She sang "Happy Birthday" with tears in her eyes and that night in bed she wept bitterly in his arms.

14

Peter called Cooper's office and spoke to the receptionist. He said it was about arranging medical treatment and, using an assumed name, he made an appointment with her.

Porlock had appealed to him and it was as P. Porlock that he arrived for the meeting towards the end of the next day. The receptionist was standing, clearing her desk, almost ready to go. She handed Peter a small piece of paper with an address on it.

"Mr. Cooper is sorry but he wasn't feeling well this afternoon and went home early. He just called to say you could still have your meeting but at his home."

"Oh, I'm sorry. He doesn't want to postpone?"

"No, he tries to give priority to appointments of this type." She smiled and repeated, "It's okay. Really."

Peter took this to mean that the police had been alerted to the meeting's change of location and that they had him covered. He drew a deep breath.

"Right. Thank you."

The address was nearby: a newish condo. Cooper's place was near the top. He'll have the best view, thought Peter, and rang the bell.

It took some time before the old lawyer answered the door and Peter could see he did look unwell. His face was grey and lined, his tremor pronounced.

"It's you? I don't want to talk to you." He began to close the door.

Peter tried to put desperation into his voice. "Wait. It's our little girl. My wife is panicking that she won't receive a kidney before she dies. She's not doing well on dialysis and the stress is affecting the whole family." He lowered his voice. "You said you could do something about her position on the organ list?" He looked hopefully at Cooper.

"Porlock, eh? Hah. I know my Coleridge. You better come in." He stood aside to let Peter enter.

"But do you know your Stevie Smith?" asked Peter, alive to the absurdity of the situation: a sick, old man and a middle-aged English professor seemingly about to barter for a little girl's life. "She welcomed the Person from Porlock 'To break up everything and throw it away.'"

Cooper raised his eyebrows, then said, "Sit." With a sigh of satisfaction Cooper sat down in a comfortable chair facing the lake. The view was indeed fine: Toronto Islands on the left, where, from time to time, a plane took off from or landed at the airport; to the right, an open expanse of Lake Ontario, endless as an ocean, on which tiny sailboats shimmered. Cooper sipped at a glass containing a clear liquid. He didn't bother to offer Peter anything.

"So you want me to move your kid up the list. What's her name?" Peter said it. "Annie. So Annie is to go up the list while others wait. Where are your ethics now, professor?"

Peter flushed. "My wife... It's hard to watch the child fail and feel helpless." He waited.

Cooper drank. "Well, I lied. I was bluffing. I have nothing to do with any waiting list."

Peter felt a spurt of anger and sprang from his chair, his composure vanishing. "You bastard. All because you want to control Eleanor's public image. Unbelievable." He headed toward the door but Cooper stopped him.

"Wait." Cooper rose and shuffled to the kitchen. Peter heard the sound of a glass being refilled. Cooper reappeared and sat back down. "Wait." He drank thirstily. Peter returned to his seat, smelling the gin as he passed by Cooper.

"I meant to say I have no access to any organ recipient list in Canada." He emphasized the word 'Canada' and smiled.

Peter groaned. "You've got to be kidding. Are you suggesting a foreign organ transplant? Please tell me we're talking about India: poor people selling a kidney."

Cooper's face settled into a look of bitter satisfaction. "Funny, isn't it, Forrest, how life plays tricks on us? You, the new activist, seeking to use the very system you take pleasure in criticizing. And look at me — access to any organ I might need, but do I get a disease where one would set me up? I do not. An inoperable brain tumour." He looked down at his glass. "I wonder if they'll be transplanting brains in a few more years. Too late for me, anyway." He drank. "My heart's no good, either."

"I'll say," Peter muttered under his breath. "So if not India, where?"

"Why, China, of course. China, where corruption is endemic and they have so much human life the rules are different. That's all. Different rules. A different game. Want to play?"

Peter sank his head into his hands, then looked up. "I don't have a choice, do I?"

Cooper laughed. "Oh, you always have a choice, Forrest. It's just the consequences that most people don't want to think about."

"I'm not taking Annie back into China. There was some irregularity with her immigration. I can't risk it."

"Oh ho, not so squeaky clean after all. Not a problem. A kidney is viable for between twelve and twenty-four hours. You can fly to somewhere else in Asia and the kidney can be flown to you. It just costs extra. How much is your marriage, your child, worth to you, Forrest?"

"How much do you charge?"

"I? I am just the broker. I take a percentage of the hospital's fees. That's both hospitals — the donor's and the recipient's. Contact my secretary for the amounts." He waved his hand. "Go away, Forrest. I'm tired."

"But why? How did you begin? Why do you do this? You don't need the money."

"You wouldn't understand. I do it because I can. Because I can."

"I don't care if you're tired or not." Peter leaned forward. "We're not finished."

Cooper smiled. "Not yet finished with me, Mr. Porlock? Now, what could that mean?" He placed his glass on a side table and stared at Peter with a slight renewal of interest.

"What if I can't afford the operation? What about that, eh?"

"Then you're out of luck and your kid is out of luck. Finished."

"What if I have something to trade, some information?" Peter was improvising wildly.

"I'm listening. Information about what?"

"The deaths of Eleanor and Bill. Their murders. What if I know something the police don't know?"

Cooper's eyes narrowed. "Oh, yes?"

"I found a letter. A letter from Eleanor to me."

"I gave you the letter Eleanor wrote to you."

"You gave me a photocopy of a letter typed on Eleanor's typewriter. But did she type it? Or maybe what you gave me was part of a longer letter that you edited, rewrote and retyped? Anyway," Peter finished, rather lamely, he thought, "I found another one, a rough draft of the letter you tampered with, in one of her books."

"And?"

"And…in the letter, Eleanor suggests that you are running an organ brokerage as well as receiving kickbacks from pharmaceutical companies in return for introducing them to the right doctors at the right hospitals — military hospitals, in most cases — where they might conduct tests, drug trials, using human subjects."

"Is that all? Transplant tourism is not illegal in Canada — not yet, anyway. And I may be a consultant for one or more pharmaceutical companies. I have the expertise they need. As you also know, consulting is not illegal."

Peter spoke the next words all in a rush. "Eleanor felt threatened by you, physically threatened."

"Did she?" Cooper stroked the side of his jaw with one hand. "Suppose, for a moment, I pretend to believe you, Forrest. That there is a letter, that it says what you say it does and that you've not yet shown it to the police. Why haven't you shown it to the police?"

Peter stuttered, "Wh — why, I didn't know if any of it was true. I couldn't see why you would do such things. And you were still her lawyer when she died. She hadn't fired you."

"No, she hadn't. I'll have to see this letter before we proceed with any deal. Where is it?"

"It's in a safe place." He hurriedly added, "And not at my home, so don't bother harassing my family. It was you or your gang who sent the pamphlets and made the phone threats."

"You astonish me, Forrest. It sounds more like the work of those faithful to the Chinese Communist Party line than of an entrepreneur like myself. Bring the letter to my office and we'll talk. Now go. I am really very tired." He closed his eyes.

Peter let himself out. He felt dissatisfied. Cooper hadn't incriminated himself regarding the murders of Eleanor or Bill. He drove home and that night, after supper, started to rewrite Eleanor's letter.

The next morning he went out early to water the garden. He adjusted the hose nozzle and sent a gentle mist over the half-inch-high carrot and radish seedlings, then a stronger sprinkle among the already sturdy peas and lettuces. He should begin supporting the peas with branches and sticks: construct a funky, homemade trellis. The broccoli transplants were doing well. He flinched at the word "transplants," wondering at the murky world he'd wandered into, where people were discarded as easily as he might pull up and discard a weed.

He began to coil the hose, then thought better of it and left it on the lawn. The weather was predicted to be hot for the next few days. He'd need the hose again sooner than later. He went into the basement and carried outside the trays of eggplant, peppers and tomatoes: all the tender plants that still needed to harden off. He put them on the north side of the house in the shade and went in to breakfast.

Jenny was popping toaster waffles for herself and the others, pouring syrup, even cutting Annie's waffles for her. She's really coming along, thought Peter.

"Who's a good girl, helping her sisters?" He kissed the side of her head and saw a small smile briefly appear. "Where's Mummy?"

"Mummy's sleeping," said Liza, chewing a waffle energetically.

Peter frowned. "That's not like her." He put two more waffles in the toaster and went upstairs. Sure enough, Jan was curled on her side, sleeping. Peter went back down to the kitchen, ate his waffles and came to a decision.

"Who wants to come to Toronto with Daddy today? We'll visit a nice lady in a big house, then we'll go to Toronto Islands and check out the amusement park."

The girls cheered.

"What about Mummy?" Jenny seemed concerned.

"Mummy deserves a day off. Now go get ready."

Jan woke up while everyone was brushing their teeth and choosing what to wear and wandered into Annie's room where Peter was preparing her for the trip.

"What's going on?" She rubbed her eyes.

Peter eased Annie into a sweater. "What's going on is I'm taking these monkeys to Toronto. Get them out of your hair. It's a beautiful day. Why don't you take a lawn chair and a book outside and relax?"

"I think I'll just go back to bed. Where are you going?"

"I have a bit of business to do at Dot's, then I thought we'd head over to Toronto Islands and fool around on the rides there."

Jan yawned. "I'm burnt or I'd offer to come with you."

"No, no, the whole point is to give you a quiet day alone. And I really need to see Dot. Enjoy." He kissed her and left.

Entering Toronto by Kingston Road, he pulled into a drive-through. While waiting for the order, he called Dot. She was home. Fifteen minutes later they pulled into her driveway.

Cream tulips were blooming alongside purple alliums in the perennial beds that fronted the house. As he unloaded the girls, Peter wondered if Dot did the gardening herself or had professional help. The gardens had all been freshly edged, the soil turned. "Be careful of the flowers, Liza, Jenny," he called as he walked toward the front door with Annie. Maybe bringing the kids to Dot's immaculate house with its delicate, aged furniture hadn't been such a good idea.

Dot welcomed them gracefully and made weak tea for the girls to drink with their doughnuts. When the three girls went into the backyard to play, Peter was relieved to see mostly lawn with surrounding shrubs. Evidently Dot hadn't yet planted her annual flowers. Dot got them playing badminton as Peter went to find Eleanor's typewriter in what had been Bill Hyde's study. Dot said it had been in its box since they'd cleaned out Eleanor's apartment a year ago.

Peter opened the box and put the machine on Bill's desk between the photocopier and a pile of bills and bank statements. He plugged it in, inserted a piece of paper and pecked. Whew! If it hadn't been working or had needed a new ribbon, his plan would have been delayed. He took his copy of Eleanor's letter to him as well as his rough draft of a variation on that letter from his pocket and studied the contents.

Shouldn't be too hard. He'd use that and that and imply the fear she may or may not have felt of Cooper here. It didn't have to be perfect. Among her comments about dissidence in China and forced organ donation, he included a description of the Chinese man he'd seen at Cooper's office and, in vague terms, implicated him. That'll rattle Cooper's cage, he thought.

He made a photocopy, found an envelope and called to Dot out the kitchen door.

"Got what you need?" she asked. He'd told her they were trying to goad Cooper into some risky action or trick him into confessing Eleanor's murder.

"I hope so," he replied.

On the way to the Toronto Islands' ferry, he dropped the new letter off at Cooper's office.

The girls adored the ferry trip. They went on rides reserved for little kids, of course: spinning teacups, a mini-rollercoaster, and the merry-go-round. Standing next to Annie, holding her on her painted horse, Peter felt his heart expand in enjoyment of the day. They had some hot dogs and hamburgers for lunch, walked around a bit until they were tired, ate ice cream sitting on grass under a big tree and boarded the ferry back to the mainland. All three girls slept on the way home. After supper Peter dozed on the sofa while a rejuvenated Jan put them to bed.

"How did it go?" she asked.

"So much fun," he mumbled, not bothering to open his eyes.

"Well, I gathered that. I meant, your plan."

His eyes popped open. "Oh, that. Just wait and see, I guess. See what he does next."

What Cooper did next was predictable. He emailed Peter, telling him to make an appointment through his secretary for Annie to see a doctor. It was what he did after that that was surprising.

15

Peter unbuckled Annie from her car seat and let her run toward the house. He followed wearily with her diaper bag. They'd been at the dialysis unit since eight that morning. Keeping Annie amused and still while her blood was mechanically cleansed was exhausting. A shocked-looking Jan appeared in the doorway.

"What's happened?"

She put her hand on his shoulder and, as Annie pushed past, said, "It's Cooper. He's dead."

Peter's jaw dropped. "You're kidding! What happened?"

"Smythe called around ten. He wants to talk to you. Peter, I'm really scared. Three people dead and just you left. You and Dot."

Peter pulled her close and felt her body trembling. "But don't you see? This may be a good thing. Maybe Cooper was the murderer and has killed himself. Let me call Smythe."

"He said he'd be busy all today and would call you tonight. And about Cooper being the murderer of Eleanor and Bill, that's what you said about Bill when he was found dead — that he had killed Eleanor and then killed himself out of remorse."

"Well, maybe Cooper died naturally from his tumour. We'll have to wait to hear what Smythe finds out."

That afternoon, as Peter cut grass and watered the transplants waiting to go into the ground, his mind kept seeking the right juxtaposition of three elements — Eleanor, Bill, Cooper. It was like a combination lock to which he had the three numbers but no idea of their order. Inspired by Dot's neat front garden, he edged and dug his own, thinking about Jan's comment about him and Dot, and wondered if they might be in danger. He phoned Dot, but there was no answer, so he left a message expressing his condolences. After all, the man had been a kind of uncle. Then he called Cooper's office. The secretary answered and Peter, feigning ignorance of Cooper's death, asked for a medical appointment for Annie. The woman gave him a time, date and location, then paused. "You'll be dealing directly with Dr. Que from now on," she said.

"Oh?"

"Yes. Mr. Cooper died last night so his partner, Dr. Bian Que, will be taking over the business."

"I see. Can you give me some idea of how much money we're talking here?"

"A kidney is usually around $75,000 but Dr. Que told me to tell you that he would honour any arrangement you had with Mr. Cooper." Her voice took on extra meaning as she added, "You did have an arrangement with Mr. Cooper, didn't you?"

She's warning me, Peter thought. "Yes, yes, I did. He was going to pay for the medical side of things. I was going to pay, still am, for our airfares and hotel rooms. So that's still on, is it? Good. Well, thank you very much." He paused. "I'm sorry about Mr. Cooper."

She commented drily, "Yes, it's unfortunate. Goodbye, Mr. Forrest."

"Goodbye."

That night, when Smythe phoned, Peter put the phone on speaker so Jan might listen too.

"His secretary called the police when he didn't come to work or answer his phone this morning. Smith and I had a look before they took the body away. Pills and gin, or pills dissolved in gin. The autopsy will tell us more. Apparently he was pretty sick, in pain. We have a good lead, though: we're pretty sure Dr. Bian Que visited Cooper at his condo last night." He paused as Jan made an exclamation. "What? You know the guy?"

"Peter just made an appointment to take Annie to be examined by him," said Jan with tension in her voice.

Smythe continued. "Huh. Right. Where was I? Yeah, there are security cameras in the condo entranceway and in the elevators but not in the halls. So we can't prove he went to see Cooper, but how else did he get into the building unless someone living there let him in? He better have a good story."

"Did Cooper have a copy of the fake Eleanor Brandon letter at his place?" Peter asked.

"We haven't finished looking but so far we didn't find it."

"Do you think Dr. Que took it?" Jan was leaning forward when she asked the question and Peter was relieved to see she looked her usual bright-eyed self again. He gave her a smile.

"It's a possibility," Smythe replied. "I just thought you'd like to know he's in the picture rather more than we previously thought. You'll be seeing him soon then?"

"Yeah. A consultation, an examination of Annie, and then, I guess, the referral process will kick in. I'll tell you if I pick up on anything while I'm there."

"Thanks. See you." Smythe rang off and Peter and Jan looked at each other.

"Wow," said Jan. "Strange, eh?"

"What?"

"Well, if Cooper killed Eleanor and Bill and was getting away with it — I mean, he thought he had a deal with you — why kill himself?"

"Just feeling rotten?" Peter suggested.

"But you said he enjoyed the power of his dealings, controlling people's lives. What made him suddenly give all that up?"

"Maybe it was an accident. He was drinking a lot when I saw him. He took a pill, forgot he took it and took another. And so on?"

"Maybe." Jan didn't sound convinced. "Do you think Dr. Que killed him?"

"It sounds like he was there. Why would he kill Cooper? Maybe their partnership wasn't working. One of them got greedy. I wonder what kind of man he is?"

"You'll find out soon enough."

Peter parked in the lot behind the Davisville medical building and walked around to its entrance on Yonge St. He remembered he'd had a dentist in this building years ago when he was a kid. He checked the listing in the lobby. Look at that! Klein was still working. He must be in his seventies now.

Peter found Dr. Que's suite number and held Annie so she could push the button to summon the elevator. She was wearing a little red-and-white-checked dress with matching frilly white shorts and white sandals. They looked at each other in the elevator's mirrored walls. "You sure are pretty today, Annie." He lowered his face to her clean and fluffy hair.

Suite 1310 was all the way at the end of the hallway, so it was into a corner office full of light that Peter stepped. Two other people were waiting in the reception area: a middle-aged Chinese couple. They looked blankly at Peter and Annie, then away.

Peter filled out the form the pleasant secretary gave him. So much family history they'd never know about Annie. He wondered if her parents were living or her grandparents.

The middle-aged couple went in to see the doctor. Peter handed the form back to the secretary and she began entering Annie's information into her computer. After the Chinese couple left, the secretary got up and left the office, giving Annie a quick smile as she passed.

Peter's nervousness increased as they waited a few more minutes. It was very quiet. The walls must be soundproofed, he thought. Finally, Dr. Que appeared at the doorway between his offices and reception and led them through.

His office was nothing special. No window, grey walls, neon lighting. He sat at his desk, looked at some papers and cleared his throat.

"I received the file for your daughter from her family physician and also from the hospital where her kidney was treated, then removed." He coughed. "I think she is a good candidate for a transplant. Based on these notes, it would seem she had an earlier transplant but the body rejected the organ." He looked up. "Correct?"

"As near as we can guess, that's what happened. We're not sure. She wasn't on any drugs when I adopted her last year so it all came as a surprise. Is it normal in China to do a transplant and expect the body to accept the kidney without drugs?"

"The donor would have to be an almost perfect match, say, from a twin, and even then there would be a chance of rejection."

"A twin," Peter wondered aloud. "We never thought of that."

"It's unlikely." Dr. Que leaned back in his chair and put his fingertips together. "You have to understand, Mr. Forrest, that in China most transplant donors and recipients are matched based on blood types alone and this doesn't narrow the donor field the way tissue-typing does. So, better for recipients as more possible matches. But bad for recipients as more immunosuppressant drugs are required to help the body adjust to foreign tissue."

"Is that the kind of match Annie would get — based on blood-type alone?"

"Yes."

"I see. So lots of drugs for the rest of her life?"

"Not necessarily. Lately researchers are finding people can decrease the amounts or stop some drugs completely, but gradually, over time. And each case is individual. We never know."

"And the organs come from executed prisoners who have consented to donation?"

"Absolutely. I myself have witnessed these executions. Very humane. Like putting a sick pet to sleep. I will examine your daughter now."

He led the way across the hall to an examination room. Light filtered through sheer white blinds and reflected off white-painted walls.

Peter sat Annie on the examining table. It didn't take very long. Dr. Que made a few notes regarding her scars. They returned to his office.

Here we go, thought Peter. "About the payment and where we'll do the transplant…"

"I understand Mr. Cooper was prepared to offer the medical expenses gratis. I will honour his wishes." Que looked down at his desk. "For the same consideration."

"You've read Eleanor Brandon's letter then? You believe Cooper killed her because she threatened to expose his unethical affairs, ruin him in Canada?"

"I don't say I believe and I don't say I don't believe." Que's eyes hardened. "I have a good business here. My children are safe. They go to the best universities. I mean the best. And this is expensive. I don't want anything to happen to my business." He looked down at his hands. "Not just me but other partners are concerned." He gripped the edge of the desk. "You should be thankful I have argued with them in favour of treating your daughter instead of finding some other solution." Peter's eyes widened.

"Are you threatening me?"

"Don't be stupid, Mr. Forrest." Que relaxed and his tone softened. "You will stay outside of China—somewhere in Malaysia, perhaps—and the kidney will be brought to you." Peter nodded. "My secretary will contact you with the name of the travel agency and the hospital in whatever city we decide to use. That is all." He rose.

Stunned by the conversation, Peter mumbled goodbye and left. Annie whimpered by the elevator when he absentmindedly pushed the down button himself. When the doors opened, they met Dr. Que's secretary coming back from her break. She had her lunch in a white plastic bag and smiled and waved bye to Annie as the doors closed. He let Annie push *G* for ground.

Peter didn't feel he had learned anything new. That Dr. Que, a respected transplant surgeon working in a major Toronto teaching hospital, was part of the same syndicate as James Cooper, which sent people to Asia for expensive organ transplants, seemed obvious. No specific information of the origin or quality of organ. No guarantee that the aftercare would be high quality or even appropriate. A risky business indeed — for the recipients. Peter thanked God that Annie was stable and managing on dialysis, not some poor patient who was nearing the end and desperate for one last chance at life. Sitting in the car, he wondered what he should do next. He called Smythe.

"Nothing much to report. Que is just the medical gatekeeper at this end of the process. He'll pass me on to the travel agency and then the hospital in Malaysia. I mentioned the letter and he didn't blink an eye except to remind me I should be grateful he and whomever else he works with hadn't been forced to find another solution. I'm still not sure if he was threatening me or referring to Annie having or not having the operation. Did you find the letter?"

"No, but that doesn't mean anything. Cooper was as likely to have destroyed it as Que was to have taken it. Forget the letter. Oh, yeah, the pills were dissolved when Cooper ingested them, which makes us lean a little more towards murder."

"Not if he didn't like swallowing pills."

"Thanks, Forrest. You're a big help."

Peter grinned into the phone. "No charge. So I'll leave it up to you guys then. Let me know if I can help."

"Will do."

Peter and Annie reached home after lunch. As he told the others that they'd stopped for chicken and chips on the way, both he and Jan paused, waiting to see if Jenny would be jealous of Annie's treat. She hardly seemed to hear them; instead, she was full of excitement about playing outside at school instead of doing work in the classroom.

"I can't believe you're almost finished kindergarten," said Jan. "Imagine going into grade one next fall. I'm so proud of you, Jenny."

Jenny preened. "I can almost read," she boasted.

"You almost can," agreed Peter. "And Liza knows her ABCs and her numbers, don't you, Liza?"

Liza took up the challenge and recited first the alphabet and then all the numbers she could remember as well as a few she made up. She had just got to twenty-eleven when the phone rang.

"Me again," said Smythe. "What do you know about offshore banking?"

"Nothing personal, I assure you! Only what I read about in the news. You need a lawyer or lawyers, many dummy companies to push the money through and an ultimate destination far, far away."

"You also need megabucks, because all that handling costs money. And it's usually done either because the money is dirty in the first place or to evade taxes."

"So?"

"So we've found a lot of incriminating documents that suggest Cooper and Que and — get this — Bill Hyde were moving money like crazy. Too bad two of the three are dead. It looks like we've got at least a tax fraud case. Maybe we can take down a few of Que's silent partners when we get him."

"So I won't be hearing from Dr. Que regarding our phony transplant trip?"

"Nope." Smythe sounded cheerful.

"But you still don't know or can't prove that he murdered any of the three victims, can you?"

"No." Smythe's voice lost its optimism. "No, we haven't any evidence against him. Not yet. Thanks for reminding me."

"Never mind. Hopefully he'll be out of circulation for a long time."

"Hopefully. But I bet he can afford the best lawyers."

With that, Peter said goodbye and went out to the garden to weed. Carrots needed thinning too. He was kneeling, back to the sun, enjoying its warmth, when a memory came to the surface of his mind. He sat back on his heels and thought for a moment. He'd better make sure.

16

Telling Jan he had to wrap up the year's work at the university, Peter drove first to Ruth's house. As he had been earlier, Ruth was gardening. She looked up with anxiety as he got out of his car. "Anything wrong, dear?"

"No, no, Ruth." He looked with affection at her pleasant face, so like Jan's. "We have had a hard time of it, haven't we? This past year — you've been great. Can I ask you another favour?" She nodded and he produced a piece of paper. "After I leave, just call this number and tell them I've gone to this address."

"That's it? Why don't you call them yourself?"

"It's a long story. It's to do with Annie's bogus transplant."

"Well, all right."

"Thanks. And one more thing. Could you, if you're talking to Jan today, maybe not mention I was here? Only if you happen to be talking to her."

Ruth's face looked doubtful. "Are you asking me to lie to my daughter, Peter?"

"Not lie, just forget." Lamely, he added, "I don't want her to worry."

"Ah-hah! Why should she be worried? I don't like it."

"Please, Ruth. It will all be over soon. All the deaths, the police. I think I can end it. Just call that number and don't tell Jan." He got into the car. He could see Ruth staring at him as he backed up and drove away. In the rear-view mirror he watched her go into her house.

When Peter arrived at Dot's, her son Max was throwing a basketball through the net mounted on a giant stand at the side of the driveway.

"Wow," said Peter. "Pretty nice. Is it new?"

Max looked down at his feet and mumbled, "Yeah. Mum got it for me."

"Are you good at all sports, Max? I know you play hockey."

"I'm okay." He looked up. "I liked what you wrote about Grandma, in the book. She was great."

"Do you miss her, Max?" Peter asked gently.

The boy said, "Yeah," then turned away and resumed sinking the ball in the net.

Peter walked up the path to the front door. The creamy tulips were browning at the edges, turning inward as they wilted. The alliums were still erect and fresh-looking but their tiny, delicate purple flowers had become round, green seed heads.

"Peter! This is a surprise. Come in." Dot looked at her son before ushering Peter through the front door.

"He seems a great kid," he complimented her. "He was just saying how he misses Eleanor."

Dot caught her breath. "Oh, he is, he is. Since Mum's death, and his father's, he's been getting quieter and quieter. And now with James dying — not that they were close — it brings back memories of the others, you know?"

"I know. Listen, Dot, I was on my way to work and I wondered if I could just check something I saw in one of Eleanor's boxes, some papers I thought I wouldn't need but now may. If I write her biography. May I have a quick look? It shouldn't take long."

"Of course, Peter, whatever you need. I'll be in the kitchen. You know the way."

Once in the study, Peter went right to one of the boxes marked "Eleanor — papers," picked it up and brought it to Bill's desk. He took off the lid, took out some papers and spread them out on the desk. Then he turned to what he'd really come for.

Like Jan, Dot wasn't fussy about filing her household papers and had a pile of receipts, bills and bank statements stacked on her late husband's desk. A heavy wrought iron paperweight held them down. As he picked it up, Peter noticed the rusty object had CPR stamped on it, the letters in relief. He wondered if Bill had been a railway buff.

He laid it aside and flicked through the pile. Phone bill, electric, oil, monthly statement for Dot's personal account: she had that much in there? Peter's eyebrows shot up. An invoice from a landscaper. That answered the question of whether Dot did her own gardening. Ah. Here was what he'd noticed the day he typed Eleanor's fake letter — a statement of quarterly earnings from stock investments with the portfolio broken down on subsequent pages. Yes.

"You're looking in the wrong pile," Dot said pleasantly from the door. She came into the study and offered Peter one of the two glasses of lemonade she was carrying. "I thought you might like something cold," she said as he took a sip. She smiled. "I added just a little bit of gin."

"Delicious," he said politely, putting the glass down on the desk.

Max poked his head around the door, looking anxious.

"Max, darling, go get yourself some lemonade. Fresh made."

Max disappeared and they heard the front door slam. "Kids," she said, rolling her eyes.

"Yeah, kids," Peter agreed.

"Get what you need, Peter?" She looked shrewdly in his face as he answered that, yes, he had. "Good. How's Annie? What a cutie!"

Peter was surprised. "Annie's fine. Why?"

"Oh, I thought you were worried about her. I must have got it wrong. She's doing well on dialysis? Now, who could have told me otherwise? Of course. It was James."

Peter looked calmly at her. "I was exploring options in case her health takes a turn for the worse." He added sweetly, "But thank you for asking."

The front door opened and closed and they heard Jeana call, "Mum, where are you? Mum?" As Dot's head turned, Peter, saying a silent "Forgive me, Eleanor," poured most of his drink into the box of Eleanor's papers and replaced the lid, praying it wouldn't soak through the cardboard and leak onto the desk.

"In here, sweetie. You're home early. What's up?"

"I didn't feel well so I skipped last class. Hi, Mr. Forrest." With apparent difficulty, she favoured him with a brilliant smile. "I'm going to lie down."

"I'll be up in a minute to check on you, Jeana."

"You love your children a lot, don't you, Dot?"

"They're everything to me. Everything. Where were we?"

"You were going to tell me about your business with James Cooper."

"My business? Oh, you've finished your drink. Want another?"

"Sure, Dot. Why not?" He held out his empty glass.

"Why don't we sit outside on the deck?" She motioned him ahead of her. He pretended to stumble a bit as he moved through the study doorway, steadying himself against the wall as they moved down the hall.

Dot laughed. "I don't know if I should let you have another drink, Peter. You go ahead outside."

As he meandered toward and collapsed onto a chaise longue, Peter saw Dot was watching him through the kitchen window. When she brought him his second glass, he let it slip almost from his grasp before taking another sip. "James Cooper," he muttered. He saw she'd put on her mother's bright blue sweater.

"James was a smart man. He'd been advising my father and mother, as well as Bill and I, for years. I trusted his judgment. If James said something was a good investment, it was."

"Was Bill amenable to taking James' advice?"

"Bill was a good-looking idiot. Not only was his money sense terrible, he was stealing to hide his mistakes; moving money from one client's account to another's, trying to stay ahead. After the bank figured it out, he only kept his job because of my family's position and Cooper's influence."

"Your family's reputation is important to you, isn't it, Dot?" Peter pretended to sip from his glass then put it on the deck on the side hidden from Dot, spilling some through the wood slats as he did so.

"The Brandons have been important in Toronto for a hundred and fifty years: businessmen, politicians, philanthropists. My father was born in this house." She looked down into her drink. "I'm not going to lose it."

"But what about your trust fund and your job, Dot?" He took a deep breath as he prepared to gamble. "You told me you got rid of your questionable stocks. Didn't you have enough without taking more from frightened, sick people, to say nothing of the people being exploited in China?"

Dot laughed. "You're so righteous, Peter. My trust fund has diminished as the economy has diminished. I doubt when he locked it in thirty years ago that my father would ever have thought interest rates could go so low. And I've never done more than teach one course a semester. Again, family influence. We practically built the place. I think the university liked having a Brandon teaching for them, just not too much." She added bitterly, "I don't even have tenure. No, I had to do something."

"So when James suggested you join him in the tourist transplant business, you jumped right in."

"You couldn't argue with the profits. And Bill and I, like James, knew the kind of people who could afford to buy themselves a new kidney or liver."

"And then Eleanor found out."

Dot's face fell. "Yes. Bill's fault. He was bragging. She was sorrowful, disappointed. She suggested we sell the house — retrench — and get out of the business with James." Dot's voice took on a wondering tone. "She said money wasn't important."

"But it is important to you."

"I couldn't have our whole way of life change because she didn't approve."

"You spoke on the phone."

Dot's voice rose in a wail. "She said she was going to change her will." Peter watched her struggle to calm herself. "She was going to disinherit me and Max and Jeana because of her ideals. I begged her to wait, to reconsider, but she hung up. I went over to her apartment right away. She'd already taken the sleeping pills and was trying to tape the plastic bag around her neck when I let myself in. I could see an envelope addressed to James on the table so I opened it and read it quickly. She kept saying, 'No, Dot, no. Leave it alone.' I ripped it up in front of her eyes, then helped her finish her task." She shuddered and briefly closed her eyes. She reopened them and Peter felt the force of their glare. "It was her own fault. She shouldn't have tried to deprive my children."

Peter made his voice faint. "And Bill?"

Dot waved one hand impatiently in the air. "Oh, Bill. Useless. Almost from the beginning. My father knew. We never spoke of it but he knew.

"Bill thought I was losing my mind. That was the only way he could rationalize what I'd done. As soon as I told him about Mum I knew it was a mistake. He started to drink more heavily than usual. He made a fool of himself when you were here for dinner. I was afraid he'd blurt it out to the children or to James. No, I don't regret killing Bill, just marrying him in the first place."

"But he was the father of your children." Peter tried to rise but fell back limply.

"Exactly, my children. I cared for them, I studied their needs, catered to their abilities, gave them my full attention. What did Bill do? Almost lost them their good name and then most of their money."

"Did James know about you and Eleanor or you and Bill?"

"You mean did he suspect that I killed them? James was a lawyer. He never asked a question to which he didn't already know the answer. So if he suspected, he knew which questions not to ask. Mother's death suited him: she was going to fire him anyway. I don't know if she'd have tried to expose details of his ventures in China. Maybe. As for Bill, I don't suppose James cared. He dealt with Bill as a courtesy to me, a family obligation, if you like. Maybe he thought I got Bill to murder Mother and that Bill then felt guilty and took his own life." As Peter tried again to rise, she asked, "How are you feeling?"

"My mouth and tongue feel numb and I feel so weak. What's happening?"

"I'm afraid you're going to have an accident, Peter."

He tried to shout but wound up whispering. "Accident?"

She put an arm under his and pulled him to his feet where he stood swaying, looking stupidly at her. "Come on." She supported him carefully down the steps from the deck to the lawn and around the side of the house. Max was still shooting baskets and looked worriedly at them.

"Is he sick?" he asked.

"Just not feeling well," replied Dot. "I'm going to drive him to the hospital. Help me get him into the car, would you, dear?"

Max's eyes bulged with excitement or fear: Peter couldn't tell. "Mum, Mum," the boy stammered.

"Just help me, Max," Dot snapped.

A white Crown Victoria pulled up to the curb, blocking Dot's driveway. As Peter straightened and backed away from her, Max put himself in front of his mother. Smith and Smythe got out of the car. Dot turned and began to run back to the house when the front door opened. Jeana stood there screaming, "Mum, Mum" over and over. Dot collapsed on the steps while her children stood helplessly.

Dorothy Brandon-Hyde was arrested for the attempted murder of Peter Forrest.

"Then what happened?" A fascinated Jan fixed Peter with her gaze.

He topped up their wine glasses. "Then we all went down to the police station, told our stories and filled out forms. Dot was held without bail and her kitchen was searched. The same narcotic James Cooper had in his system was found. The dregs of my glass and what soaked into the cardboard box I'd poured the first glass into are being analyzed." He drank some wine and smiled at Jan. "That's better. Got to get the taste of that drug out of my mouth. The police suspect it's Cooper's painkillers stolen by Dot."

"What about Max and Jeana?"

"Both terribly shocked, of course. I think one or both of them may have suspected their mother of finishing off their father. That would explain their exaggerated behaviours toward me whenever I saw them. Max was always surly, unwilling to look me in the eye. Jeana became hyper-cheerful, perky. I don't think they thought Dot had killed their grandmother."

"Now they have lost both parents. So sad."

"Yes. Max is eighteen but Jeana still needs a guardian. I believe some Hyde relations have stepped forward. And there's sure to be some money for them even after the criminal allegations are settled. I suppose I'm going to have to waste some of my sabbatical going to court to testify against Dot. Smith and Smythe are going to be busy, trying to find evidence to support the other charges of murder they want to bring. It's my word against hers. But as she lied about visiting her mother the day she died — visiting her twice — and was caught on camera at Cooper's condo the day he died, she has some explaining to do."

"How did they find out she visited Eleanor twice?"

"The elderly neighbour who was moving her furniture into the hall the day I met Cooper at Eleanor's place. She saw Dot coming into the building and then arriving again later when the paramedics were working on Eleanor. She forgot to mention it."

"Forgot?"

"Yeah. Good thing Smythe reinterviewed her. So Dot visits two people who shortly thereafter turn up dead, not to mention Smith and Smythe always liked her for Bill's death. Apparently," he grinned at Jan, "apparently, it's often the spouse."

"Hah. You're lucky I don't kill you for taking off on such a foolish mission. What if she'd just conked you on the head?"

"It wasn't her style. Or the murderer's style, if it had turned out not to be her. Remember, I only suspected she'd lied to me about her 'ethical' stock portfolio. My suspicions grew when I read the list. Among the pharmaceutical companies, I saw the ones I know are investing in China's transplantation research and development and which are almost certainly turning a blind eye to abuses of prisoners there."

"What's happening to Dr. Que?"

Peter smiled and said with relish, "He's being audited. And he's been told not to try to leave Canada. Let's hope they get him, fine him and lock him up."

Jan shuddered. "I can't believe we let such a person examine Annie." She thought for a moment. "Peter, would you fly to far-away places and spend your last dollar to get her a chance at life? Or me? Would you do it for me?"

Peter groaned. "Oh, honey. I've done the research. The outcomes in individual cases just aren't good enough to risk it. It's like taking your car to be serviced at night or on weekends by the guy who works out of the alley behind his house. There's no accountability if bits of it fall off later. Annie's doing fine. We have to be patient. She'll get her kidney."

"I hope so." She scratched her head. "So Smith and Smythe didn't know why you'd gone to Dot's and you didn't know about Eleanor's neighbour's new testimony or about the security video of Dot at Cooper's. Why didn't they tell you?"

"I guess they thought I'd be more effective if I only had a vague suspicion. When they got my message from Ruth, they were all set to go. Poor Max. They're pretty sure he noticed someone watching the house all afternoon. That's why he stayed out front with his basketball. He was trying to guard his mother."

"Speaking of mothers, I've already had a word with mine," Jan said grimly, "and told her never, ever to do such a thing again. If something had happened to you, how would she have felt towards me? You put her in an awful position."

"I know, sweetheart. I'm so sorry. But you've been struggling of late, what with Jenny and Annie, and I couldn't put that on you as well." He leaned over and kissed her. "Forgive me?"

APPENDIX

Poems

by Eleanor Brandon

&

Peter Forrest

Poems by Eleanor Brandon

The Key

The key must enter the eye many times
If the eye blinks the key cannot turn
Hold steady

One Daisy

You have to think about one daisy
There it is next to the path
A field of daisies yes
You have to think about that too
But one daisy
Think of that

Strange

that one red leaf
among so many green
resembles an apple
animals have
a resistance to
this fraud
survival
demands
that some
still reach out
and taste.

Small Poems to the Chinese Government by Peter Forrest

'One daisy ... think of that.' Eleanor Brandon

Don't close eyes. Might meditate.
Don't stretch. Might become supple.
Don't relax mind — might open.

White coat takes your blood.
Prison guards give beating.
Exchange of money.

White van. Red cross.
Sound of motor running—
sometimes screams.

Snowflakes fall into water—
easily absorbed.
Are they gone?

Harvest day — hospital—
gurneys lined up.
Doctors joke: good practice for students.

Neurosurgeon—
takes four thousand corneas over two years—
looks into his own eyes.

Corneas, kidneys, liver—
skin peeled off—
precious beating heart.

Body numb. Heart paralyzed.
Brain alive.
What is pain?

A tree grows, obstructs your way.
Prune it? Cut it down?
No. Make a new path.

AUTHOR'S NOTE

I first became interested in the issues swirling around international adoption when a good friend of mine adopted children from China. While I knew that China's one-child policy had resulted in the abandonment of many babies, the majority of them girls, I really had no knowledge of the staggering numbers of orphans, or the conditions they lived in. And then I learned about suspicious organ "donations" from prisoners. I wondered if I could construct a scenario where these two themes — surplus children and forced organ donations — might intersect. Three books which were invaluable in my research into these issues were *Bloody Harvest: The Killing of Falun Gong for their Organs* by the international human rights lawyer David Matas and longtime human rights champion and politician David Kilgour (Seraphim Books, 2009), *State Organs: Transplant Abuse in China* by David Matas and Dr. Torsten Trey (Seraphim Books, 2012), and *Losing the New China: A Story of American Commerce, Desire and Betrayal* by Ethan Gutmann, Ethan (Encounter Books, 2004).

ABOUT THE AUTHOR

Born in Montreal and raised in Hudson, Quebec, Louise Carson studied music in Montreal and Toronto, played jazz piano and sang in the chorus of the Canadian Opera Company. She currently lives in rural Quebec, where she gardens, teaches music, and writes. An award-winning poet, she's widely published in literary magazines from coast to coast. Her poetry collection *A Clearing* is published by Signature Editions. *Executor* is her first mystery.

Eco-Audit
Printing this book using Rolland Enviro 100 Book
instead of virgin fibres paper saved the following resources:

Trees	Solid Waste	Water	Air Emissions
2	106 kg	8,660 L	348 kg